D0000361

5 Centimeters per Second
one more side

Story by Makoto Shinkai
Adapted by Arata Kanoh

Translated by Kristi Fernandez

VERTICAL.

5 Centimeters per Second one more side

First published in Japan in 2011 by
KADOKAWA CORPORATION, Tokyo.

English translation rights arranged with
KADOKAWA CORPORATION, Tokyo.

Published by Vertical, Inc., 2019

ISBN 978-1-947194-09-0

First Edition

Vertical, Inc.
451 Park Avenue South, 7th Floor
New York, NY 10016
www.vertical-inc.com

5 Centimeters per Second
one more side

Chapter One
On Cherry Blossoms

17

Last night, I had a dream about the past.

I'm sure it's because of the letter I found yesterday.

I feel like I should have given him the letter that day, after all. This lingering feeling now compels me to write.

I will be trying to describe what happened when I was a young girl.

But I'm not so sure I can do it. It's because I'd given up on conveying anything beyond words in the first place that I couldn't hand him the ones I'd penned.

I guess I'm a bit hesitant because I might belittle my experiences of that day by writing them down.

Still, I probably ought to have given it to him. For the first time in ages, in over ten years, I read over the letter that I wasn't brave enough to part with, and my young self made me smile.

I was able to feel generous.

You should have given it, I wanted to go back and tell the me of that day. Too bad I couldn't have been more forgiving about my own immaturity and imperfection.

In that sense, what I am about to write is a terribly belated letter.

I mulled over this, but I'll start with my school transfers.

I can get self-conscious over trivial matters, and having trouble telling people where I'm from is one of them.

In a diverse city like Tokyo, establishing where you're from is an important way to break the ice; however, I always get a bit flustered when the topic comes up.

According to my parents, I was born in Utsunomiya.

But I don't remember living there. I don't think of it as my hometown. Since my mother's side of the family is from Utsunomiya, it sometimes comes up in conversation at home. Even so, I never really feel one way or the other about it.

My family and I moved to Akita before I started elementary school. Then, we went to Shizuoka Prefecture, followed by Ishikawa Prefecture. We moved around because my father, who worked at a regional electronics manufacturer based in Tochigi Prefecture, had to transfer to branch offices in various areas for his job.

For that reason, even to this day, I still don't feel like there is one set place where I belong.

When you repeatedly move and change schools as a child, that tic tends to take root in the very base of your consciousness.

Wherever I went, I never made myself comfortable.

To me, every new place felt nothing but temporary and impermanent.

This was my general attitude, ever since my earliest years and throughout my adolescence.

It was the winter of third grade in Ishikawa Prefecture.

When my mother told me that I would be changing schools the following year, for the millionth time, I was a little glad to escape from Ishikawa, but terrified of starting all over again.

"Next will be Tokyo!"

My mother made it sound like we had hit the jackpot.

Looking back on it now, we probably *had* hit the jackpot in terms of my father's career. Yet I felt nothing but a growing ominousness from the creaky sound of the name "Tokyo."

At that point in my life, I had never once felt emotionally attached to a school, a town, or even a person, and I had the vague sense that things were doomed to be that way forever.

I once read an essay by someone who had repeatedly changed schools when he was young, just like I had.

The writer claimed to clearly remember and feel connected to every single town he had lived in.

But I had no leeway to do that at all. If I let my eyes roam around, I would make eye contact with someone.

Whenever I made eye contact, words came hurling at me.

Those words were almost never kind. I would always keep my head hung low and try my best to avoid confronting anything.

I felt scared every time I had to change schools.

New places and strangers did not make me happy.

No matter how many times I transferred, I could never fit in at a new school.

I was genuinely terrified of everything: of the fact that I was the only one who spoke with a very different intonation, of the unique viscosity of bonds in each locale, of the unfamiliar buildings and people, of the unfairness of everyone else in class knowing one another when I did not know any of them.

Whenever I was thrown into a new place against my will, a shrinking sort of feeling spread over my skin.

My classmates' slightest gestures and offhanded words only put pressure on me.

While I wish I could have hid my fears and pretended I was fine, I wasn't strong enough to do something that difficult.

Fear is a sign of weakness.

In the immature world of children, weakness is nothing but a target for malice.

I felt sick every day, all the time. The shoulder-jerking nausea was constant.

If I just feel a little worse, I won't have to go to school, I would think. Then my nausea would become even more intense.

But awkward moods and tense atmospheres, I could endure.

As long as I breathed softly, trying to take shallow breaths, and tightened my skin, time would automatically pass me by.

It was the cruel words I couldn't handle.

I couldn't cover my ears. If I did, they would have shouted even harsher things at me.

There are a few words I can't stand to this day. I was surrounded by the type of words that kids love to use for bullying. There were times when even my *teachers* used them.

By then I already knew that adults, too, turn into immature children amongst them.

I thought I would have to spend the rest of my life, until the day I died, simply waiting for the time to pass, but I couldn't figure out a way to escape.

In fact, the very idea that I *might* escape never occurred to me. All my younger self could do was stay silent and let others push her around.

The only thing that comforted me was reading.

I could immerse myself in glorious worlds all alone. How did something so wonderful even exist?

I still feel that way.

My heart could safely reside somewhere else. That was what saved me.

When I opened a book, I could become another person. I could dive into different lands and experience unbelievable things. The scenery that I gaze at with my mind's eye is always more brilliant than the ones my physical eyes see.

I spent my days in the real world taking shallow breaths behind closed doors, always with my heart in that imaginary world. I learned all sorts of things from my books.

At that time, when I was a third grader in elementary school to be exact, I was smitten with C. S. Lewis' *The Lion, the Witch and the Wardrobe*.

A world deep within a wardrobe, mythical beasts of the Sun, an evil Snow Witch lurking in the shadows... I was enchanted by the images that unfolded in my head. I dreamed about that world and never grew tired of it.

I opened and closed my own wardrobe many times, of course, even though I knew it wasn't the entrance to another world.

Every time I opened the book, it felt like I was opening an imaginary wardrobe's doors to send my mind to the other side (Lewis must have been aware of this "opening" analogy).

The only place where I truly belonged was always behind the door of my imagination.

When my mother announced that we were moving to Tokyo the following spring, I clutched my book's hard, solid cover and desperately tried to suppress the feeling that new horrors were coming my way.

I already knew too well what would happen.

I would be forced onto a platform, surrounded by my amused classmates, who would inevitably go from interested to disappointed, leaving only a terribly oppressive air around me.

I never dreamed of fighting back, nor did I know there was a door through which I could escape. I held on to the special place in my imagination, simply enduring the pain from the outside world in order to protect my little domain.

A desperate patience was the sole theme of my nine-year-old life.

My environment intensified my fears, and my fears only made my classmates treat me worse.

I thought that this vicious cycle might follow me until death, which is why I never felt like I "belonged" anywhere.

I must have been wearing my usual gloomy stare when my father's old car pulled up to our new apartment in Sangubashi, Tokyo.

I hadn't even glanced at the passing scenery on the way. I couldn't care less what the new cityscape looked like.

I would just end up with the same bitter taste in my mouth.

It was about to start all over again. The panic and pain inside me would only bleed one shade deeper as though an additional layer of paint were being applied.

My temple leaning against the car window, I wished a wall, transparent and strong like the window glass, would always protect me.

So the *slam* of the opening car door sounded really eerie.

When I got out of the car, the parking lot's asphalt feel beneath my shoes and the penetrating, chilly air made me want to cry.

Very soon—in just one week—a new academic year was going to begin, and I would have to go, alone, to a totally unfamiliar place.

When I imagined it, the pit of my stomach tightened and released a toxic fear that spread through my body to my fingertips.

Back in those days, I think I was in the habit of vaguely contemplating death.

Deep down, I knew I couldn't live like that forever.

But I didn't especially want to die. I wasn't brave enough to kill myself, of course.

I imagined that, if the bitter feeling persisted, I ought to grow weak, crumble little by little, and see my shadow fade—and then I would vanish instantly, like a snowflake.

That prospect didn't bother me at all. What a relief it would be if my breathing and heart just stopped and my consciousness disappeared along with the pain, I would think with my still immature mind.

And that was when and where I met Takaki Tohno.

15

The height of the lectern always made me feel dizzy.

Even though it was only four inches off the floor, the mere sight of it made my heart sink and gave me the shakes.

A swarm of eyes was watching me. Each individual face swayed and shifted restlessly.

I couldn't figure out what lay behind their faces and deep in their eyes.

I heard a giggle come from somewhere and reflexively hunched my shoulders. Then I lifted my interlaced fingers up to my chest.

Startled by the sudden *screech* of chalk against the blackboard, I turned around.

They were laughing openly now, and I felt more and more like I wanted to get out of there.

After the teacher finished writing "Akari Shinohara" on the blackboard, she placed her hands on my shoulders and turned me back towards my classmates. My shoulders only stiffened under her hands.

This is Akari Shinohara. She'll be studying with us from now on. Let's welcome her to our class.

After the teacher spoke, she gave me the cue to say it was a pleasure to meet them. I bowed while I spoke, and my voice cracked. The air in the classroom seemed to buzz with criticism.

"What a weird name," someone said. The entire classroom practically ruptured with laughter.

People always made fun of my name when I transferred to a new school, so I had ended up thinking that it was actually strange.

The teacher scolded the student, but only halfheartedly. Even adults overlook problems in order to keep the peace.

Even though I was too young to wrap my head around many things at the time, I was perfectly aware that my teachers weren't my friends.

She gestured to my seat. I hadn't noticed how stiff my knees had become until I got off the platform, and they almost gave out. My legs trembled as I staggered between the desks to my seat.

I wondered why my body wouldn't just move how I wanted it to.

The girls and boys on each side of me lowered their heads and their eyes and turned in their seats to watch me pass by.

The brush of their gaze against my trembling hands and swaying skirt made my body so tense that all the pores on my body seemed to be sealing shut.

My vision was closing in and I lost focus.

Everything looked like it was wavering.

Why does my seat feel so far away? I thought.

I hung my head lower and lower.

And then…

A whispered voice entered my ears.

"You are going to be okay."

Surprised, I reflexively straightened my back. Up until that moment, I hadn't noticed how lousy my posture had been. My distorted vision instantly cleared up.

I wanted to stop and glance around to find the source of the voice, but there was no way I could. I made my way to my seat in the back-most row.

Many students turned back to look at me. I would have normally stared nervously at the grains of my desk, but my eyes swam over my classmates' faces.

Who?

Who whispered that to me?

The words had been so quiet that I began to doubt I had actually heard them.

And in fact, I was the only one who was reacting to the whisper. No one else had noticed the voice.

But it was a boy's…or at least that's what I thought.

Even after the teacher tapped on the lectern to get our attention, I simply kept gazing at the level rows of black hair.

After first period, my classmates stared at me for a good while, then slowly began to crowd around me.

A big group of them circled me and released their rapid-fire questions: *Where are you from? Why did you transfer here? When is your birthday?*

I was so preoccupied trying to find the owner of "the voice" in the sea of faces that I couldn't give a decent answer to most of their questions.

You are going to be okay.

That remark was still echoing in my head.

The words intrigued me.

What exactly did they mean?

They echoed in my head until they became a string of indecipherable sounds.

My mind went fuzzy.

It was as if I were under a spell.

To be honest…

They were the words I had always wanted to hear.

I know, now, that I vaguely wished for them every time I went somewhere new.

The perfect words that my nine-year-old self sought without knowing what they might be.

Someone had understood my anxieties.

And sympathized with me.

The idea of having a secret friend…

Enchanted me.

That one whispered remark had given me a supportive push and helped me lift my face.

For some reason, the transfer felt much less scary than usual.

A girl who looked strong-minded, most likely a leader of the bunch, kindly misread why I was glancing over their faces with my eyes wide open, unable to speak properly.

Assuming that the group had startled me, she told them to give me some space and stop asking their nonstop questions.

I was shocked; my halting speech was just the usual, but she had taken it in such a positive way. It wasn't long before I figured out why.

Ah, everything is so different if I just raise my head…

That was the first day at a new school I had ever enjoyed.

I found the voice's owner later that day.

I was spending some of the breaks between classes glancing around, and my eyes suddenly came to a stop. I knew I had found him.

While a nice group of girls told me about our other classrooms, I stole glances at him.

He was chatting with his friends as if it were just another ordinary day. The boys around him acted the way students typically do when there's a new transfer; with evident excitement, they snatched glimpses of me, tried to eavesdrop on my conversation, and seemed to be critiquing me.

Essentially, students react to a new transfer in one of two ways: they either show great interest or reveal a more perverse curiosity by feigning total indifference.

Yet that boy seemed to have a different reaction altogether.

He stood there looking neither interested nor disinterested, sort of neutral, or absentminded.

At that moment…

I think I viewed him as a totally different being, unlike any other person.

His oddness was clear to me.

At first sight, he fit in naturally with his surroundings. There was no mistaking, however, that he stood at a remove.

It was as if a wall as thin as a single sheet of paper separated him from his surroundings.

It was as if he existed in another dimension by that thin layer, unbeknownst to anyone.

I was very interested in this boy. Or rather, only he interested me.

I wanted to find a way to stand before him and get a better look at his face. I wanted to ask him his name.

But a transfer student couldn't do that, couldn't express her interest in just one of them. Even quietly asking someone wasn't an option. Transfers were expected to make friends with the entire class, to swallow it whole.

That day, after school, a few girls walking home in the same direction invited me to join them.

It was incredibly rare for my first day to end in such a calm and friendly way. My heart raced with joy.

Walking with the group of girls, who didn't seem to hate me, I thought about the boy the entire time. I wondered how I might learn his name.

As we proceeded along the wall around the school, we came across a cherry tree that stood just within its border. Wind-swept cherry blossoms gently rained from its branches, which were beginning to turn green.

It was usually at the start of spring semester that I transferred, but I think that was the first time the trees and flowers really caught my attention.

Five centimeters per second, I said to myself.

My father, who has a childish side, sometimes came home from the bookstore with a science magazine for elementary school kids that he used to subscribe to as a young boy.

In one of the issues, I had eyed a piece of trivia in the margins that tickled my fancy: cherry blossoms fall at a speed of five centimeters per second.

For every notch of a clock's fastest hand, a cherry blossom falls two inches closer to the ground.

And what would be my speed, in getting close to him?

I'm not sure if I came up with that metaphor as a child—but now that I am an adult, my memories from that day exist between an image of falling cherry blossoms and the phrase "five centimeters per second."

14

After a brief time, I learned that his name was Takaki Tohno.

My teacher had given me a list of my classmates' names, saying it would be better for me to memorize them sooner rather than later.

I asked a girl who liked to go out of her way to help people to match each name to a face. Remembering everyone's name was just a pretense, though; my real aim was to learn his.

Until that point, I was honest to a fault and never thought I could act contrary to how I felt. That I could was a brand-new discovery for me.

I knew his name, but that was it. I wanted to get close to him, but couldn't imagine talking to him.

I didn't know how to approach him, and if I did so out of the blue, I would stand out and summon a flood of judgmental glares, and then something terrible would happen. My head overflowed with all the ways it could go wrong.

To begin with, I had nothing to talk about…

What's more, I was afraid of boys.

A certain image of them was etched into my mind: rowdy, loud, given to awful words and deeds.

The villains from my books acted extremely nice at first—I might have made such an association.

So I avoided looking at him, but also always kept him in the corner of my eye.

It was after a month or two that we spoke for the first time.

Classes, cleanup, and homeroom had wrapped up, and I went to the second-floor library at the end of the hallway.

The school library supposedly had a policy against educational manga, so all of the books only contained words. Hardly any children want to read books without pictures. That wasn't always so, I have heard, but it was already the case in my time.

Which was why I had the books all to myself.

There were student library assistants, but since they were rarely at the checkout counter when they were supposed to be on duty, I would always stamp my own library card and take out the books by myself.

When I entered the silent, empty library, I naturally hushed my breath and tried to mute my footsteps.

Ready to return the book I had borrowed, I took the card out from the stock that still lay on the front desk, stamped "returned" next to my name, and headed to the shelves to put the book back where it belonged.

When I passed through the rows of bookcases and was just about to reach the last one, my body completely froze—and so did my head.

Takaki Tohno was there.

Facing the spines that lined the shelves, he was focusing on a spot just above him.

But I suspected he wasn't actually looking at the spines.

He seemed to be looking *through* the bookshelf—if the books and shelves had been made of glass, his gaze would have been vaguely focused on something on the other side.

All of the spines lining the bookcase, which faced the southern windows, had faded to a lovely yellow from the sun.

The low, faint evening light shone in through the windows and onto Takaki's back.

The downy hairs on the nape of his neck shone gold in the light, and his shadow had spilled across the spines of the books.

I was as still as a figure cut in stone, gazing at this picturesque view.

When I snapped out of my trance and tried to make a run for it, he noticed me and turned around.

"Um…" a rasping voice caught me from behind, and my body went stiff.

I couldn't move.

I could hear the sound of my own heartbeat.

My body was calling for an emergency shutdown. I wasn't sure whether I was scared or hopeful.

"Akari Shinohara?"

Hearing him call my name, I became even more flustered and tried again to flee, but my legs wouldn't budge. I shrank behind the book I held in my hands as if to shield myself.

"Are you returning that?" he asked.

"Huh?"

"Can I take it out next?" he said gently, easily…and when I saw him pointing at the book in my hands, I felt totally helpless.

His unassuming, absent eyes squinted in the light of the setting sun. With an unlocking, echoing *clink*, the first tier of my defenses came down inside me.

At first, I think I only ever responded to him by quickly shaking my head or shrinking back into silence.

But…

"I also just transferred here. Last year."

The moment he revealed that to me, my heart practically leapt out of my chest.

He had repeatedly changed schools like me.

First he was in Nagano, then Mie, and finally he had come to Tokyo via Shizuoka. I had also lived in Shizuoka.

He spoke in a leisurely and adult-like manner, and his voice was reserved. He always stopped to think before he spoke.

He never acted out and made me recoil or said dirty things like the other boys. I felt comfortable enough to listen to what he had to say.

The two of us sat beside each other, against the library wall beneath a window, and talked about the things only transfer students could understand.

I nodded many times as I listened to his stories, and he did the same as I awkwardly stumbled through mine. *That's so true*—thoughts that we had wanted to give voice to streamed out of our mouths in turn.

From this story to that, he was sure to understand everything I had to say.

Which is why I found myself naturally bringing up all sorts of topics.

For the first time in my life, I knew how nice it felt to have someone nod and say, "I know how you feel."

With surprising ease, I told him all the things I had never been brave enough to say.

The light outside gradually sank lower, and grew redder, and settled on the bookcase before us as if to further bleach the sun-kissed books.

By the time we reluctantly waved goodbye at a fork on our ways home, it was dark out—and we had become really, really close friends.

The more we talked, the more we realized we were surprisingly alike.

23

I guess being a transfer student had given us similar traits.

We both liked to read books. More specifically, we liked reading much more than throwing a ball around, hanging off the jungle gym, playing a game that someone just thought up, or pretending to be interested in boring conversations.

We both knew how wonderful it felt to slowly nurture and expand the world in our hearts.

In certain situations it is better to spend time by yourself. He was the first person who had ever agreed with me on that.

He and I were both pretty frail. We both had to stay home from school or sit out during gym class numerous times.

This had probably fostered our tendency to ponder things in silence.

When the tendency manifested as a disconnect from others, both of our parents had taken us to see psychiatric counselors. We also both eventually stopped seeing these doctors after we moved.

We even excelled in the same subjects: language studies, history, and science.

We did exceptionally well on our language studies tests, though we didn't like that class at all.

We both despised the way our teachers guided us through questions that had very specific answers.

Takaki and I also had our differences, of course.

He had a far more calculated approach to fitting in at school.

He would joke, fool around, and abruptly stand up to other kids to secure a foothold in their society.

He tried to hide that he didn't fit in even as he protected what he truly valued.

I think I was the only one who noticed that about him.

I found his method both shocking and refreshing. I thought I might be better off if I acted like that, too...

As the type who always cowered and silently backed away every time I faced something, I was surprised by his efforts to be social, and it made him seem dependable.

We started having long phone conversations without telling our parents.

When that wasn't enough for us anymore, we started spending every moment, even at school, together.

It felt completely natural.

I never knew how desperately I needed someone who understands me. Through Takaki, I was able to integrate into a new elementary school.

I had adapted to my new environment and been accepted. It was an incredibly rare and precious experience for me.

I felt free, as if a weight had been lifted off my shoulders. Those were the first days in my life that I wasn't afraid.

"I wanted to talk to you ever since you transferred here."

When Takaki admitted this to me, I felt fulfilled.

Most girls in elementary school hope to someday find their true love, or, to use an old expression, they believe in the "red thread of fate."

Until then, I had never wished to find my true love or anything like that. I never thought that anyone would ever love me.

That was my understanding of life and the world.

Thanks to Takaki, I think I felt normal emotions for the first time in my life.

In other words, it was because the boy I always liked had always cared for me—it was all thanks to that miracle.

Takaki and I spent most of our time together in the library.

After school, we would stand next to each other and gaze at the shelves. Then we would carefully choose a book, sit across from each other at a big table, and read to our hearts' content. Sometimes one of us would hear the other giggle and react by peering into the book and pointing at an illustration. We were always taking out some sort of book.

At that library, I read stacks and stacks of books.

That was where I read the entire Narnia series, from *Prince Caspian* on.

Takaki recommended I read *A Wizard of Earthsea*. Takaki preferred Ged when he acted serious in the second half, but I also liked when he was unbearably arrogant in the first.

Momo. The Little Prince. The Neverending Story (it was tough lugging that book all the way home!).

Takaki liked Arsène Lupin, and I liked Sherlock Holmes.

Garden in the Sky by Judith Worthy.

The Flying Classroom.

The King Series by Teruo Teramura.

Shinichi Hoshi's books for kids.

I made Takaki read *Anne of Green Gables*, so I had to read *The Fiend with Twenty Faces* in return (it was pretty scary).

In retrospect, it was the perfect selection of books for the young kids that we were. It warms my heart to recall these memories after all this time has gone by.

Whenever we read each other's favorite books, it felt as if I had built a bridge to the little world in my heart and exchanged with him everything I had inside it.

Every time we read the same book and he told me that he liked a part I had missed, I felt like I was learning something new about him.

13

Nearly a year of these perfect days had passed.

It was evening, and I was walking home alone from school. We couldn't stay glued together 24/7, so I sometimes walked home by myself when we weren't able to meet.

I think it was around the middle of May, when I was in fifth grade.

It was a lovely day, where the tender warmth of the sun could almost soothe you to sleep.

Tempted by the pleasant weather, I felt the urge to take a detour.

Since school was right near the boundary between Setagaya and Shibuya, I would always pass the Yoyogi Hachimangu Shrine on the way home.

The shrine sat at the top of a small hill, which was so packed with trees that it looked like a neat arrangement of parsley.

I usually just saw it in the corner of my eye as I went by, but that day I suddenly decided to climb the long staircase to the shrine. I wanted to see what was at the top of the hill.

I climbed the steps, one by one, sliding my palm up the steel handrail and feeling the hard stone beneath my feet.

Rows of tall trees created a tunnel of leaves and branches over the staircase. The higher I climbed, the more the trees dimmed the light overhead.

I arrived at the top of the staircase and went through the *torii*.

There was a gentle curve in the smooth gravel path to the shrine. Red lanterns dotted both sides of the path.

A sacred tree covered the road with its foliage, as if it were its roof. Sunshine poured down between the branches, creating patches of light on the ground.

It was there I saw Takaki.

I had run into him completely by chance.

He sat on a large rock on the side of the path and was gazing into the distance. Slightly bent forward, he almost looked like he was sleeping.

He was as still and quiet as if he had turned into one of the rocks or the trees.

There were two cats next to him, one on each side.

They were stretching, lying down, sitting up, twitching their tails. Looking away from him all the while, they nonchalantly attached one portion or another of their bodies to him.

Takaki and the two cats were simply there, each facing a different direction.

Despite facing in their own directions, they somehow seemed to be communicating through telepathy.

All touching and connected.

Specks of sunlight rained down through the leaves above their heads.

The gentle wind occasionally brushed them as it passed.

I marveled at the scene before me. It was as if I, too, had turned to stone.

It felt like God was trying to reveal to me an important truth, as if a fragment of the universe's secrets had been laid out in the picture I beheld.

"There's also an Ibi River in France…"

I jumped, startled by the voice.

Before I knew it, Takaki had noticed me and turned his head in my direction.

"The Ibi River?" I asked.

"You know the Ibi River here, in Japan?"

"Um, the one in Gifu Prefecture?" I said with a lingering sense of surprise. Takaki had actually lived near Gifu, in the Chubu region.

"Yeah. I was looking at an atlas in the library today and found another Ibi River in France. Pretty neat, huh? Maybe there's another Tama River somewhere in the world."

"Does that mean the world is all connected?" I asked, offhandedly.

Startled by my question, Takaki gazed fixedly at me.

"You know, I've never thought about that before."

He looked around at the leaves that obscured the sky, the concrete *torii*, and the paved path to the shrine.

"I think it must be," he murmured, sounding convinced.

With an admiring look, Takaki stared straight at me again. He still seemed to be digesting the vague question I had asked.

I was growing more embarrassed by the second.

Takaki had a habit of staring.

All I had done was blurt out a question that had popped into my head. I didn't know how to react to him mulling it over or taking it to heart.

No one had ever taken my words so seriously, and I was at a loss.

I always took what people said too seriously. It had never been the other way around.

Takaki averted his eyes. He brought his hands close to the cats, almost touching them.

"Mimi is the white one and Chobi has the brown spots," he said.

"Are they siblings?"

"Hmm, I'm not sure. But they're always together."

I crouched down near Mimi and reached for the back of her neck. Mimi's fur was as fluffy as down.

It was enchantingly soft.

The friendly white cat rubbed her forehead against my hand. After two or three more rubs, she abruptly stood up and sprinted across the path. Chobi yawned lazily and followed after her.

A strange feeling still lingering inside me, I arrived home, jumped into bed, and brought the blankets over my head.

I thought about the Ibi River of a faraway land.

I wonder what it's like.

I bet it's a lovely river on the smaller side.

But I don't think it's a shallow stream. It bet it's narrow, but deep. The flowing water is dark, and kind.

The choppy surface would shimmer in the light of the summer sun.

That was how I pictured a river I had never seen, in a country I had never been.

Then, leaping out of bed, I headed to my desk and took out a notebook from the drawer. It was just an ordinary school notebook.

But also one of my most treasured possessions.

I have a strange habit. I enjoy writing down bits of trivia that I acquire from books and TV programs.

I had crammed loads of facts into my notebook. For example, how moles need to eat their weight every day in order to live; how half of the seven thousand existing languages will disappear in one hundred years' time; and how the Pont Neuf, which translates to "The New Bridge," is actually the oldest existing one in Paris.

I had just about finished filling my third notebook.

Only much later did I realize that I had been trying to protect myself in this way. Gathering knowledge was how I drew nearer to the secrets of the universe.

I surrounded myself with information to try to comprehend "the way of the world."

It was my childhood ritual—an attempt to somehow figure out the "answers" to the eternal secrets of the universe.

I started a sentence on a new line in the notebook:

"There is an Ibi River in both Japan and France."

Then, after some hesitation, I added another sentence in tiny letters.

"That's how the world is all connected."

Right, I should show Takaki my notebook at school tomorrow.

He's going to be so stunned and impressed.

I bet he keeps all sorts of facts in his head. Or maybe he even keeps a notebook like me!

At the same time I had that thought, I felt so overwhelmingly embarrassed and awkward, and in the end I never showed him my notebook.

12

I want to write about one more thing that happened in fifth grade.

If I could say that no noise interfered with the time and space I shared with Takaki, and that peaceful days continued forevermore, it would be an absolute fairy tale...but that, of course, was not the case.

We were on the verge of puberty, and our classmates were at an age where they began to notice our relationship.

Takaki and I were really close. The two of us were always together.

I guess that really roused our classmates. They just wouldn't stop teasing us.

It was during a long break, so it must have been lunchtime. A group of boys came up to me and jabbed me in the shoulder. The ritual teasing began.

When's the wedding? And more direct questions.

While I can laugh about it now, it felt like absolute death at the time.

I tried talking back to them but instead choked on my words and made a strange guttural noise. All of my classmates burst into laughter.

I felt goose bumps forming on my upper arms, and my blood ran cold.

Takaki wasn't there.

They had carefully planned to attack when they knew I would be alone. Their spite scared me beyond belief.

When Takaki wasn't with me, I would return to my old helpless self.

The nasty boys were getting a kick out of my inability to respond, and the problem only escalated. They went to the front of the room, stood before the blackboard, and excitedly started doodling.

They teased me and Takaki with the classic *aiaigasa*. They decorated the drawing of a shared umbrella with all colors of chalk.

Red heart marks proliferated, and Takaki's family name was appended to my first name.

Speechless and frozen in horror, I listened to my heart pound louder and louder in my head.

The growing pressure in my head was excruciating. Why does your body always shut down at such times?

After they finished their drawing and had a good, long laugh about it, I finally managed to coax my trembling legs towards the blackboard. *Next, I should reach out, grab the eraser, and drag it right across the board.* I understood that in the back of my mind.

But that was the one thing I couldn't do.

The moment I came face to face with the drawing, their will to humiliate me bore down on me, and I started to fold.

A dense, murky cloud of malice leaking out from the blackboard seemed to wrap around and cling to me.

Spite.

Malice.

It was even hard to breathe.

The boys and the laughter were nothing compared to the terrifying malice emanating from the blackboard.

I knew the Devil.

I knew that the Devil didn't just exist in the stories I read…but also in the real world.

Their will, leaking from the chalk drawing like gas, was it.

What I most feared.

What bound me with an invisible thread.

The blackboard went out of focus.

My face was on fire, my toes felt like ice.

My heart was shattering into tiny fragments. I hung my head lower and lower.

I would be crying in a few seconds.

Just then, the sound of brisk footsteps beating against the vinyl floor cleared the fog that clung to me.

My classmates went into a teasing frenzy. I was able to turn and face the footsteps. With a ferocious expression on his face, Takaki came stomping towards me.

For a split second, I was even scared of him.

When he rushed near me, I couldn't help but hunch my shoulders.

Takaki jerked his back straight up, went directly for the eraser, and forcefully shoved it across the blackboard a couple of times.

The picture, erased diagonally from the center, now made no sense. I was released from my shackles. I let out a quiet sigh of relief.

The next moment, something grabbed me. I was shocked to see Takaki's hand holding my right wrist.

Letting go for a moment, he quickly gripped my hand instead. Then I felt myself being taken away.

My body suddenly weightless.

Takaki had grabbed me and led me out of the classroom. Or rather, we had rushed out of there together, holding hands.

How can I explain how I felt at the time? It was like I was floating… I don't know how to put it, that's the only way I can describe the liberating feeling that took over me.

It was only at first that he had tugged. Before long, my body became weightless and began to move on its own.

Holding hands, we soared through the hallway.

The cheers and whistles behind us just became a gentle tailwind pushing us forward. All I felt was a sense of freedom and the firmness of his hand.

The power flowing from it, into me, made me even lighter.

The intense afternoon sunlight spilling in through the windows and onto the hallway reflected against the polished wax floor and was almost blinding.

We rushed towards the sunlit schoolyard as if to dive into the light.

It was at that moment.

I realized once and for all that I was in love with Takaki.

That was the first time I had ever held his hand. I didn't want to let go. I wanted to stay connected like that forever.

We ran to the back of the storage shed in the corner of the schoolyard. Behind the shed was a lawn with several big rock samples for science class.

We were in the school's blind spot where no one could find us just by glancing around.

We lay on the lawn and skipped fifth period. It became an issue soon enough and our teacher gave us an earful, but I remained surprisingly calm.

Takaki and I talked about all sorts of things on the grass. When there was a break in the conversation, we spent the time staring at the blue sky, and at wisps of clouds that, if you looked hard enough, were moving very slowly.

The entire time we laid there, I yearned to touch his hand again.

And, well.

I think that was the first time I ever wanted to kiss Takaki.

11

We were in sixth grade and spring had finally come.

The air was now gentle and warm, and I no longer needed to wear my overcoat.

With comments like "All the kids in Tokyo are as spiffy as they say," my mother would come home with a mound of clothes she had bought me for the spring. Even though we were going on our third year in Tokyo, she talked as if we had just arrived yesterday.

My mother is very girly, so she only bought me clothes that were frilly and cute. I was like her little doll.

Feeling confident enough to wear clothes that stood out at school was quite new for me.

I had gotten used to attracting attention. I could lift my chin and take big, sure steps when I walked.

I could laugh without caring what the other kids thought of me.

Takaki and I were spending more and more time together.

I was always by his side (or he always by mine). We were inseparable at school, and during lunch and after the final bell, we would sneak into the library's storage area, read books, and talk about them.

When we felt like we hadn't had enough time, we chatted endlessly on the phone hoping our parents didn't notice. Even the kids at school got tired of teasing us.

I would sometimes grab Takaki's hand, like I had been forgetting to.

Every time, a tender glow enveloped me.

I had been so sure that I would die unloved, and I could hardly believe that a hand that didn't brush mine aside existed.

He understood me totally.

He heard me out whatever I said.

We went on dates at various places on the way home.

If I'm remembering correctly, the cherry blossoms had budded around March 24th, then fully bloomed in less than a week.

Every time I passed Sangubashi Park on the way to and from school, the intense presence of the pink cherry blossoms seemed to grow stronger.

Happy to watch the seasons change, I often caught myself looking up at the trees.

Whenever the wind blew, the soft petals of newly budded flowers gently fluttered to the ground. It was a blissful sight to behold.

Sangubashi Park, located on a small hill in the middle of a residential area, was like a playground enclosed by trees. A narrow road, only wide enough for Kei cars and bicycles, winded around the park on its gentle descent towards an Odakyu Line station.

The cherry trees extended their branches over the road, creating flowered eaves that hung in the sky.

Although the park wasn't part of the school-approved route, I practically dragged Takaki through it so that we could walk under the cherry blossoms.

The blue sky peeked out between the clouds after the rain. The sunlight had started drying the dampness from the road.

Takaki and I walked side by side beneath the cherry trees.

Branches reflected in the puddles. Fallen petals cast ripples in the water.

Maybe it was because of the rainfall that had ended at noon, but countless petals were strewn across the lawn like confetti.

Through the cherry petals shone a pink light, onto a roadside water tower.

Even the air smelled pink.

The branches spotted the road that we walked with their shadows.

"Hey, they say it's five centimeters per second," I remarked abruptly.

"Hmm? What is?"

The bewildered look on Takaki's face gave me butterflies in my chest.

"A cherry petal falls at that speed. They say it's five centimeters per second."

"Huh. You sure do know a lot, Akari," Takaki replied distractedly.

Didn't Takaki know? Didn't he know how mysterious it was that rigid numerals could express natural movements that shook your heart?

It was so precise, it sounded like fate.

Five centimeters per second.

I think they were subtle words of love that my unconscious had pronounced.

They meant that I felt so natural when we were together.

That I always wanted to be with him.

I hoped we could, very gradually, get closer over time.

At the speed of a falling cherry petal. Slowly, but surely.

I wished that we would naturally become one.

On that day, I think my existence was the most blessed of all, enveloped in the most beautiful thing in the world.

Of course, I didn't know that when I uttered the phrase "five centimeters per second" at the young age of eleven.

But I had put all my wishes and feelings in those words.

Which is why Takaki's delayed response was a bit of a letdown.

The petals rained down so fiercely that it felt like we were walking through a storm of flowers. The dramatic sight made me feel a bit giddy.

I reached out and tried to catch a petal in my hand. It lightly twirled and slipped out from my palm as if trying to escape my body heat.

"Hey, isn't it just like snow?"

"You think so?" asked Takaki. He often replied with a question.

"When petals fall in Japan, it snows on the other side of the world."

"Brazil is opposite of Japan," Takaki went off-topic again. Actually, it was the ocean near Argentina.

"Of course the earth *is* flat," I said. And with that, I suddenly took off.

I ran down the hill and through a tunnel of cherry blossoms. The shadows of the branches and the sunlight that shone between them ran alternately over my eyes.

"Hey, wait up!" Takaki's voice called out from behind me.

He was chasing after me. I could tell by the sound of his footsteps. Regardless, I ran around the curve, as if to hide myself in the shadow of the last cherry tree that lined the road.

As I ran from Takaki, I felt at peace.

I had someone to chase after me.

That filled me with such peace, and bliss.

I reached the bottom of the hill and turned the corner.

There was a railroad crossing there.

The Odakyu Line appeared to run through the very center of the residential area.

The signal started to clang. I saw that the crossing gate was slowly beginning its descent. I crossed the tracks before the gate came down.

Even though the cherry trees had cut off a while back, wind-tossed petals came fluttering on to the tracks.

Soon after I reached the other side, the gate was down. When I turned around, I could see Takaki standing in front of the crossing and the slightly wobbling, black-and-yellow-striped gate.

"Akari!"

Taken aback by the anxiety in his voice, I opened the umbrella I held in my hand. What was wrong? It was just a closed crossing gate.

"Takaki."

I spun as the cherry blossoms fell onto my umbrella.

See, it's just like snow.

"I hope we can see the cherry blossoms together again next year," I told him.

Not only next year, but also the year after that. And beyond.

Before I could add that, a deafening train came hurtling between us.

For a moment, I felt a bit uneasy. The train rushed by with a thunderous rumble. Takaki was on the other side, but I couldn't see or hear him.

That was all it took to put negative thoughts in my head.

What if Takaki isn't there anymore?

But I didn't need to worry. After the train left and the ear-splitting noise died down, he was still there on the other side of the tracks. The thick air of spring, the light of the afternoon sun, and the snow-like petals were all around him.

When the gate started rising, Takaki hurried towards me like he could hardly wait.

Drawn by his rushed steps, my legs also moved forward to meet him, in the middle of the tracks.

Closing my umbrella and shaking off the petals, I felt comforted and happy to come close to him again.

Simply being beside him was warmer than the spring sunlight.

Was Takaki reciprocating the feelings I had tried to express to him? Past the tracks, as we continued on our way home, he suddenly asked me that question.

"Where do you want to go for junior high?"

"Junior high?"

"Yeah."

I was confused. I hadn't really thought about it before.

I just assumed that I would be attending the district's.

"Your family hasn't said anything about private schools?" asked Takaki.

"We haven't really talked about it…"

Takaki let out a light hum and, in his usual dry voice, proceeded to explain: his parents had offered to send him to a private junior high and high school in the area.

"What do you think, Akari?" he quickly continued.

"Huh?"

"I was thinking we could go together."

I was caught off guard by his sudden proposition.

"W-Well, I'll have to ask my mom…"

I took a moment to think about it.

Not that many students attended private junior highs. The chances of attending the same private school as my classmates were pretty slim.

Takaki was telling me he wanted us to go to such a place, somewhere new, just he and I.

If we went to a public school, we would probably end up with all the kids from our elementary school. It wouldn't be horrible, but the teasing would still get to me.

If Takaki and I went to a different junior high together…

We wouldn't know a single person there. We would only know each other. The two of us would work together to build a new life from scratch…

The idea entranced me.

At that moment, I had a shocking realization: Wasn't it just like transferring schools? I actually *wanted* to transfer?

I wasn't scared of changing schools anymore.

It was all thanks to the warmth I felt next to me.

"That would be great," I answered.

Then, I drew just an inch closer to him.

I was convinced that his warmth would forever be mine.

I thought I was mature for my age, but I was still a child.

We believed that we would go to the same junior high and be together to the end.

In a year, I'd find out that it was just wishful thinking.

And I had been so sure I was aware that the world around me was unkind.

10

I wasn't happy with the school uniform that hung on the wall. Its fabric was brand-new and stiff, visibly heavy and tight.

I was in my new room, which was still stacked with cardboard boxes from the move. I forced myself into the uniform as if it were some sort of punishment.

I didn't want to put on my shoes. I couldn't stand the thought of stepping outside.

I knew that once I arrived at school, the entrance ceremony would begin and I would be trapped there.

I clung to the empty hope that if I just stayed in my room, a miracle might happen, that everything would work itself out.

But I couldn't withstand the overpowering tide of reality. The sheer force of the situation was slowly pulling me in.

In my uncomfortable new uniform, I put on my shoes, as heavy as weights, and started towards my new junior high.

Even my mother's sendoff felt nothing but phony to me.

I headed down the road in low spirits. The private homes soon disappeared, and I found myself on a path flanked by unflooded rice paddies. When I lifted my head, they stretched far into the distance.

Further beyond were scattered dark groves.

Where on Earth am I? I wondered, not for the first time.

I knew where I was in physical terms, of course.

I just couldn't believe I was there.

I took small, dejected steps down the path between the rice paddies.

I knew if I kept walking, I would inevitably draw closer to reality.

I began to see the overhead wires of the local Ryomo Line that ran right next to the fields. The platform at Iwafune Station came into view.

A mountain of reddish stone towered directly behind the station.

Although it wasn't much in terms of height, the steep mountain looked enormous jutting out from the flat plain.

It was called Iwafune, or "Rock Ship," Mountain because of its likeness to a boat. Iwafune Station sat at the foot of the mountain. The area around Iwafune Station was called the town of Iwafune.

It was all too simple, so straightforward that it seemed unnatural.

Using my brand-new commuter pass, I went through the ticket gates at the station and walked onto the concrete platform.

Every bit of the unfamiliar routine unsettled and ruffled me.

The texture of my ticket holder's pointed edges in my hand made me feel unbelievably nervous.

When I stood on the platform, I had a panoramic view of the rice paddies I had just passed.

Since there weren't any tall buildings, the sky looked massive.

A green-and-orange train pulled in from my right. The Ryomo Line, a small railroad that connects two regional prefectures, Tochigi and Gunma.

I was taking the train to a public junior high in Oyama City, Tochigi.

The automatic doors opened and I boarded. Even though it was rush hour, there were barely any passengers. I was a little shocked. There were so few advertisements in the carriage it almost felt lonely.

I sat in an empty booth.

It all felt so wrong...

The train's wheels rolled over the tracks rhythmically.

Why am I...

Why am I...

The words echoed in my head.

For some reason tapering out there.

A standing sign bordered with paper flowers was propped against the front gate. Written on it were the words, "Opening Ceremony."

I went through the gates.

I sat with my eyes downcast throughout the ceremony.

I went to my assigned class. I sat in my assigned seat.

The boys and girls raised their shrill voices and made an awful fuss.

Somehow, being around unfamiliar, overexcited students completely wore me out.

The rapid happenings around me felt unreal, like an illusion...

The teacher opened the sliding door and entered the classroom. My vision was blurry.

The teacher was speaking, but I had no idea what about.

The students introduced themselves one by one.

A menacing feeling closed in on me, and I almost panicked.

Compelled by some unknown force, I abruptly stood up.

I only noticed it was my turn to speak after I stood.

I heard someone giggle and felt like running away.

For the first time, I glanced around the room.

I was the only one standing. Everyone else was seated.

The height difference made me dizzy.

I felt like I was going to fall.

My classmates, some of them going so far as to twist their bodies, stared at me.

Their focused gazes were as sharp as needles.

I stopped breathing.

My heart tightened.

I was unbelievably terrified.

This wasn't just being scared.

Gravity seemed to be squeezing me from both sides, as if to wring every last ounce of fluid from my body.

I felt suffocated. I couldn't move.

The room began to spin.

Unconsciously, I hoped that someone would say something to me.

Someone did say something.

It was a dirty joke.

The class roared with laughter.

Ah, yes. I remembered very well.

This was me.

This was me when I was alone.

I can't recall if the cherry blossoms were in bloom.

9

It was late February of sixth grade when the fact that I passed the private school entrance exam ceased to mean anything.

Both Takaki and I had aced the test.

We weren't the type to fail something so important.

We had taken our acceptance letters in our hands and bumped fists like boys.

It was going to be our first experience traveling to an unknown place, just the two of us.

It felt nice, to me, to see myself so excited for once.

Having a hand to hold and going somewhere new was a happy development…

I hadn't known.

I would take in each little detail—the pristine school uniforms, the untraveled route, the unfamiliar, daunting gates—wondering in the back of my mind, all the while, how he was receiving them.

We would quietly face each other to confirm them.

It was fun imagining our beautiful future together.

"Your father's being transferred back to Tochigi."

My mother, in the middle of a household chore, casually dropped this bomb on me when I came home from school and put down my backpack.

"What…"

Unable to process her words, I mindlessly watched her patter down the hallway in her slippers. A dreadful feeling came over me and I hurried after her.

"Does that mean…"

"This will be the last time, I promise. Your father has been requesting to return to Tochigi Headquarters for quite a while now. The decision was made today. He sounded really happy on the phone. Even though he has more opportunities at the Tokyo branch."

"Okay, um…"

"He said it's about time we settle down. You know, the place where your father grew up that we put up for rent—it happens to be empty right now. Right, I should have it cleaned before the move."

"Um…"

What was she talking about?

"But I passed the private school entrance exam. I got in…"

"Ah, yes." My mother stopped in place, put her hand to her cheek, and looked at me with a troubled expression. "What should we do?"

It was the face she made when she pretended to listen to my opinion while making sure that things eventually went her way.

The topic came up a few more times at home, but my parents' decision was clear.

In short, I might as well not have taken the exam at all; they would be sending me to a public school in Tochigi.

The elementary school me just couldn't accept the nonsense for what it was.

I tried convincing them in any way I could.

But no turn of phrase can reach people who have made up their minds from the start.

They turned the tables on me and asked why I was so set on that particular school. I couldn't come up with an answer.

I had never told my parents about my special connection with Takaki.

It was too important to bring up to them.

I didn't want anything to interfere with our relationship.

Would things have turned out different if I had told them about us?

I don't think so. The end result would have been the same. Parents are loath to let go of their kids for the six years of their secondary schooling.

While I understand now, it seemed utterly absurd to the young girl I was at the time.

My head swelled with head-splitting pressure as if I had a fever.

I couldn't believe it was happening.

Yet there was my reality.

Right in front of me.

My mother's face went in and out of focus.

The wall of some dead end seemed to bear down on me.

The image of a closed crossing gate.

The side of the train, a wall rushing from left to right.

Blocked.

I got sick and had to stay home from school. As I suffered from pressure headaches, I wanted to become so feeble that I couldn't move anymore.

My vision was blurred, my skin was numb. I didn't want to think or feel a thing.

I didn't want to confront anything.

I just lay in bed and closed my eyes, shutting out all incoming information.

I kept at it for as long as I could…

But a sense of resignation slowly washed over me.

It had quietly crept in from out of nowhere and soaked into me through my extremities. It rendered my body powerless and took complete control.

Perhaps…

No matter what I tried to do, nothing would change.

No matter how I felt, I would be taken to Tochigi by force.

I finally "understood."

That understanding came to me in the form of an image. Pronounced guilty, I was being hauled off to jail.

The moment I accepted my fate, I panicked.

Takaki…

How could I face Takaki?

As if I'd had a revelation, I realized that I couldn't keep hiding this from Takaki.

It was impossible. I couldn't hide it even if I tried. If I did try, I would disintegrate from the inside out.

Then I remembered something else.

If I kept staying home from school…

Takaki would probably try to call me.

That idea scared me beyond belief.

The more time passed, the more it felt like I was being subject to some mysterious punishment.

Not being allowed to stay in Tokyo really resembled my mental picture of being thrown into jail.

That image swelled endlessly larger in my head.

If I was being punished, I must have committed a crime.

I was being punished because I was twisted and vile.

I was a bad person.

That's how I took it.

After all, hadn't I always been treated as such?

Right, I was a warped, messed-up person whom everyone thought was a joke, and I had merely forgotten that for a while.

I had to tell Takaki.

I couldn't let him notice on his own how "wrong" I was.

I mean, if he found out I was trying to hide such a thing—he would absolutely despise me.

I had to.

I had to come clean to Takaki.

I snuck out of bed and changed into my street clothes as quietly as I could. I also put on an overcoat that had a fur hood. My forehead burned against my hand.

It was already the middle of the night.

I silently went out the front door.

It was frigid outside, and I began to freeze from the feet up. I staggered towards the main road.

I was looking for a telephone booth. I was searching for one because I wasn't allowed to use the home phone at night—and also because I didn't want to talk to Takaki while my parents were close by.

I rarely used phone booths, so I wasn't too sure where I could find one.

I walked around relying on vague memories. Finally, I found a lighted phone booth next to a bus stop on the national highway.

The sidewalk was empty. Cars leisurely came and went. It felt like the overpass above my head was going to fall down and crush me.

I entered the phone booth, inserted my telephone card, and pressed the numbers on the keypad.

I needed courage to press them.

The glass booth shielded me from the wind, but it wasn't warm. I exhaled a white cloud that drifted off.

I listened to the calling trill. Every now and then the passing cars almost drowned out the sound.

Someone picked up. It was Takaki's mother.

"Um, hello. This is Akari Shinohara. Could I, um, please speak with Takaki?" I was probably talking too fast. I imagine I was nervously fiddling with the cord out of habit.

The hold music fanned my anxiety for no reason.

"You're...changing schools?"

Takaki's tone, as calm as ever, made me uneasy that day.

"What about West Middle School? You worked so hard to get in."
It sounded like he had slumped to the floor.

I could tell that he knew something was wrong.

I clung to the receiver as if I were hugging myself.

"My parents are filing the paperwork for a public school in Tochigi... I'm sorry..."

"No, you don't have to apologize, Akari."

The growing seriousness in his voice was too painful for me to
bear.

"I told my parents that I wanted to go to school from my aunt's
house in Katsushika, here in Tokyo..."

My voice grew moist. There was a lump in my throat. Welling up.

I couldn't stop it.

Takaki.

Takaki...

His name echoed louder and louder in me—

"They told me not until I'm older..."

My words, lingering in the air, shook me.

I started sobbing uncontrollably.

Water poured from my eyes.

My feet felt it trickling onto my shoes.

I was crying.

I hadn't seen it coming.

Why did my body always react before my emotions could catch
up?

My chest convulsed with gasping breaths.

I tried to dam the flowing tears.

But I couldn't.

"I get it." Takaki's voice sounded sharp through the phone. "I've heard enough."

My breath stopped at the unexpectedly chilly way he'd put it.

My body always reacted first.

There was a time lag—if my heart were a thing, I would have heard the eerie sound of it breaking.

"That's enough…" said the receiver, in Takaki's strained voice.

There was a deafening ringing in my head. My eardrums went hot and felt like they were going to burst.

My head bowed of its own accord.

I was splitting into fragments of myself.

There was my thinking self, my feeling self, and my body, which reacted independently from those selves, and also a *me* who saw everything from an objective point of view.

Each of my selves reacted differently.

They digested Takaki's voice.

His irritated voice.

Which sounded angry.

The sharp sound of it…

Frightened me.

My various selves merged into that fear.

I was scared of Takaki.

I had never heard him use that tone before.

And he had directed it at me.

I felt my blood churning.

A truck zoomed by on my immediate right, slamming the glass booth with the wind it created.

Every passing car almost knocked me over, its force too overwhelming.

I tried to say "I'm sorry," but the words stuck in my throat and wouldn't come out.

Through the receiver, which was pressed painfully tight against my ear, I could hear Takaki breathing, but the passing cars blotted it out.

When I hung up, the metallic sound that it made clawed at the back of my throat.

I clasped my hands together and realized that they were shaking.

I'm scared.

I'm scared.

I'm really scared...

Where was I directing those words?

What should I have done with those feelings?

Who should I have told I was scared?

I was all alone, in a phone booth, at night.

After that, it was awkward for a full month every time we met face-to-face, and then we had our elementary school graduation ceremony.

Once the ceremony, homeroom, and the rest wrapped up, Takaki and I had a brief conversation. We were standing in the hallway. The afternoon sunlight glistened off the polished floor.

He was wearing a blazer, which he rarely did, but I couldn't find the words to talk about it.

Unable to speak for a time, I meaninglessly moved my foot around.

"Well, I guess this..." I said, forcing a smile, "is goodbye."

I remember how dreadfully heavy the bun in my hair felt.

Judging by the way he averted his eyes...I could tell that he still hadn't forgiven me.

The raucous voices of boys sword-fighting with their diplomas' cardboard tubes came from the classroom.

I found it annoying.

I don't know if the cherry blossoms were in bloom.

I kept my head bowed so I wouldn't see anything as I headed home.

My steps grew smaller and smaller, and less and less sure. Once I was by myself, with no one around, I buried my face in my hands.

I was alone again.

I didn't have anyone.
There was somewhere.
Somewhere I longed to go.
Why wouldn't they let me?
Always…
Forced…
To move against my will.

I wished time would freeze over.
I didn't want any cherry blossoms to bloom.

8

I flipped off the switch to my thoughts and emotions, became a lifeless machine, and moved away.

After the movers loaded our belongings into a truck and drove away, my family and I boarded a train at Shinjuku Station.

We rode the Saikyo Line to Omiya. After that, we transferred to the Utsunomiya Line, then to the Ryomo Line at Oyama.

The frequent stops and endless rides forced me to realize how *far* we were going.

I gazed out the window and watched the cityscape morph into clusters of houses.

Fields then appeared between them. Before long, the houses became scarce and tapered off into farmlands.

We suddenly came close enough to the mountains that I could see the details of their surface as well as their ridgeline.

The landscape was changing little by little, and something like an itchy lump trembled and intensified in my chest, and I felt wistful.

When I first got to Tokyo I was so uncomfortable, even in the lovely residential area from Setagaya to Yoyogi. Yet before long I had grown accustomed to it and felt completely at peace.

My breaths became short and shallow again.

I looked down.

I wanted to cry because I knew it would make me feel a bit better.

For some reason, though, I couldn't anymore. The tears wouldn't come.

The only constant sensations were my nausea and trembling arms.

When I stepped out onto the seemingly desolate platform at Iwa-fune Station, in Tochigi Prefecture, my skin tightened in the chilly wind.

Out-of-season snow, which had fallen just a few days prior, clung, translucent, to the shadows on the platform.

The other side of the world. I had come to a world without Takaki.

I don't have much to say about my days in junior high.

To avoid direct contact with anything, I cautiously quieted my breath and waited for the time to pass by.

I built an invisible wall around myself and tried not to let anything beyond it affect me.

On the surface, it must have seemed like I spent my days in peace. I'd begun to grasp the importance of somehow making myself appear that way.

Still, although I seemed unaffected, some strange thing always danced in my chest. It grew fine, tiny cilia that ceaselessly attacked my lungs. At times it burst into awful jigs that made me want to give up.

I always stayed alert and listened to my surroundings.

I became sensitive to the sound of laughter.

I lived waiting for the safe passage of time.

It also depressed me to see that boys were looking at me in a certain way that they clearly hadn't in elementary school.

My mother told me I had to play a team sport, so I reluctantly decided to join the basketball club. It was something I never should have done.

I despised the pressures unique to extracurricular activities.

Like the unspoken rules that come into being.

However, I was too weak to fight back and just had to tough it out.

I think this mental block gradually isolated me from my peers.

I did everything I could to turn off my emotions. But...there were certain things I couldn't help but take to heart.

It's not right to call someone over with a whistle, but why didn't anyone recognize that at school?

Why were certain things overlooked when they would make you angry anywhere else?

Hitting a person is a crime that the police might investigate, so why did the cases go cold?

Why was everyone so blatantly nasty and vulgar?

I thought that every one of those things was wrong—but why couldn't I say it?

The words wouldn't come out.

If I could, I wanted to loose an arrow into it—and a sharp one, too.

No, it didn't even have to be words.

I just wanted to express how I felt.

There were so many things they blindly accepted. Why couldn't I tell them that it all seemed strange to me?

I felt like once upon a time, I had thrown it all back at them with a mere sigh, a flick of my eye...

I probably couldn't do it alone, though.

You need to fight fire with fire.

You need to have your own world to fight the world.

But you can't create them all alone.

Oh...

Enough of their nastiness.

I wanted something beautiful.

I wanted to connect with a beautiful heart.

I seriously, earnestly, desperately clung to that childish desire.

During those days, I think I developed the habit of talking to Takaki in my head.

I could only confess my true feelings, which I suppressed and hid from the outside world, to the imaginary Takaki. I told him this, I told him that. I told him how I felt. I confided in him using only the simplest, most honest words.

The Takaki in me would nod and say: *Yes. I agree.*

Though he never gave any specific advice, just imagining him listening and sharing my pain made my life a lot easier.

It was as if exactly half of my suffering disappeared.

7

Well into the second semester of my first year at junior high, I finally put my thoughts into action and wrote Takaki a letter.

For some reason, and for a very long time, I hadn't thought to reach out to him.

On the day of our graduation ceremony, I had said, "Well, I guess this is goodbye."

I truly believed it was our final farewell.

That's essentially what it means to change schools.

When you transfer, your previous relationships end.

Having experienced it several times, I just figured it was going to happen again.

But there was another reason I hadn't contacted him: I was scared.

I was convinced he was still mad at me.

I didn't want to face the facts.

Giving him a call was out of the question.

I was scared of talking to Takaki on the phone, without seeing his face.

His rejecting tone, from that wintry night, still throbbed like a thorn in my heart.

I had dealt with a very painful chain of events in September. I don't plan on describing them here.

I flipped off the switch to my agony and went to school. My decision to feel nothing was an effective way to cope with reality.

It seems I frequently made mistakes traveling familiar routes or found myself slumping over and leaning against something in the oddest places.

Once, I think I even missed my station by a long shot on my way to school.

I use words like "seem" and "think" because it's all just a blur to me.

One morning, I randomly vomited on the way to school. I finally admitted just how much I didn't want to go.

Every time my body involuntarily purged itself, I stayed home from school.

Calling out sick didn't mean life would get easier for me. I was painfully aware that staying home was a temporary escape.

Even now, I still think about how grand it would have been if I just escaped from it all. But realistically, I couldn't keep calling out sick. My parents and teachers would never allow it.

Escaping from the horrors for just one or two days was in fact only tiring.

It got harder and harder to just "turn off the switch."

Whenever I forced myself onto the train to school, I hated how I could feel myself slowly getting closer to it. I tried my best to think about things that made me happy.

I thought about Takaki.

In the early mornings, when there were only one or two other passengers on the countryside train, I comforted myself by filling the spacious carriage with gentle thoughts.

I could feel his aura infusing it.

I conveyed hundreds of unspoken things to him.

It was on one such day.

Sitting alone in a booth, I took the stationery paper that I used as a diary out of my bag, and finding the light pouring in through the window a little too bright, started writing a letter to Takaki… I believe another version of myself in me was looking on in utter surprise.

> Dear Takaki Tohno,
> It's been a while since we last met.

My pen effortlessly glided across the paper. Then, the surprised self in me almost seamlessly merged with the self that continued to write.

Unconsciously, I think I always knew that I would write to him someday.

> The summer here is hot, but it's still much milder than Tokyo's.
> Though, now that I think back on it, I liked Tokyo's humid summers, too.
> The melting-hot asphalt.
> The far-off skyscrapers shimmering in the heat.
> The frigid air conditioning in the department stores and subways.

As I watched my hand compose those indented lines, I retrieved my memories of the light-blue sky hanging over the swaying buildings of central Tokyo.

> It's already been half a year since we last met at our

elementary school graduation ceremony.

I counted down on my fingers and realized that it had only been months. It felt like we hadn't met in years, though, and the pit of my stomach tightened.

Hey, Takaki.
Do you remember me?

Did he? Maybe he had forgotten. We were transfer students, after all. It was second nature to forget where we had been in order to integrate into where we were now.

Although I felt scared, I decided to seal the letter.

Knowing that I couldn't rewrite or reread it made me suddenly nervous.

Even when I stuck my hand into the mailbox, ready to drop off the letter, I hesitated for a time.

I closed my eyes when I let it go.

Four days later, a reply came in the mail.

When I found it in the mailbox, my heart almost stopped.

He was *fast*.

I was happy that he had responded so quickly. That alone was enough.

I had opened our mailbox on the way home from school, but instead of proceeding through the door, I made a sharp right turn, towards the plains beyond our community.

I held the envelope tight to my chest and hurried down the path between the rice paddies.

I then came across a barely cultivated patch. I didn't know whose it was, but it looked like the crops were only for private consumption. The plot was slightly raised in the center.

And on that raised area stood a glorious cherry tree.

Of course, it wasn't conveniently in bloom.

It was a hearty cherry tree that could have gained a bit of fame if it were on public land. Its branches twisted and spread across the sky, and its enormous roots clutched the earth in every direction. Reaching out, they seemed connected to a faraway world. I adored that tree.

I sat on one of the roots of the cherry tree and read Takaki's letter over and over again.

I was surprised to see how much pressure he had put on his pencil. His handwriting was boyish and strong. A bit meticulous, too.

Having seen his notebook scribbles, I could tell he had taken care this time.

Was it the six-month gap? Maybe his penmanship had improved a bit since starting junior high.

The formal tone of his letter made me feel a bit bashful.

He must have felt bashful when he was writing it, too.

I could just picture it.

Letters are weird.

If you write in the way that you normally speak, it doesn't come out right. You tend to put on airs and become a bit stiff.

I had only written about current events in my letter, so his reply contained much of the same.

I had dispatched my words ever so gently, and he had returned his just as gently.

For me, that was crucial.

It was important that he didn't use strong words.

I didn't want to endure them anymore.

I somehow ended up losing all his letters, so I can't reproduce exactly what it said.

I can still summon, however, the impression it left on me.

Takaki's words were clean. They always had been.

He hadn't changed a bit in the past six months, I thought.

I read his letter so many times that I actually lost count. I ran my eyes, again and again, over the quiet series of sentences that simply detailed the recent happenings in his life.

I traced over the folds of his heart with my fingertip, as if it were braille—or at least that was how I imagined it in my head.

Takaki had wanted to talk to me since then…

That was incredibly reassuring.

There are scenes in old foreign dramas where a young girl, so moved by a letter she has received, hugs it tight to her chest.

She isn't exaggerating. That reaction is real.

I found out that people actually behave that way in real life. I wanted the stationery to melt and soak into my heart.

That was the start of our sporadic correspondence.

It was sporadic because I didn't want it to become like one of those exchange diaries between girls.

About once a month, we sent letters to each other about recent events in our lives. Whenever I received a reply, I felt fulfilled knowing that he had been thinking of me.

Reading his letters, I had to wonder how he was able to feel as I did—and it was moving.

I could tell that he was suffering too, but that he was doing his best where he was now.

He never used insincere phrases like "I get you" to show offhanded sympathy for my tribulations. He just casually told me what was happening in his own life.

His compassion was concealed in those accounts. That was how skilled of a writer he was.

There was a beauty to him that I hadn't known. He could compose such incredible letters.

In today's email-dominated world, missives in long hand are part of a dying culture, but they can really touch your heart.

At times, a tingly feeling would start in my chest and move up to my throat.

There's something truly affecting about a good letter.

Every time I received a response, I wrote one back.

Thank you for the reply. It made me so happy.

The word "happy" barely even scratched the surface.

But I couldn't do better in writing. It was a bit frustrating.

Takaki was still there, in that part of Tokyo, experiencing, feeling. And thinking: *I've got to tell Akari.*

I was able to confirm that much.

That alone made the days surprisingly easier to get through.

I wondered why.

Why did it feel so nice just to be understood?

Dear Takaki,

I always wrote my letters early in the morning, in an empty train booth.

It's already well into autumn.

The leaves here are beautiful. The day before yesterday, I brought out my sweater for the first time this year.

It's a cute and warm cream-colored sweater I wear over my school uniform. I really like wearing it to school. I wonder how you look in your new uniform. I bet you look so grown up...

Recently, I have basketball in the early mornings, so right now I'm writing this letter on the train.

I got my hair cut the other day.

It's so short that my ears poke out. Even if we met, you probably wouldn't recognize me.

Reading it over, I was surprised to see that I was subconsciously telling him that I wanted to meet up. But…

I'm sure you're also changing, little by little, Takaki.

Maybe I was a little scared to meet him now that he was in junior high.
I received another letter, then I wrote one back.
I think it went something like this:

Dear Takaki,
How have you been these past wintry days?
It's already snowed here a handful of times. Whenever it snows, I go to school bundled in thick layers of clothes.
It hasn't snowed yet in Tokyo, right? Even after I moved, I still check Tokyo's weather forecast out of habit.

We might meet again soon.
While I was a bit afraid, it was likely.
What sort of expression would I wear then? And what about him?
His stiff face and my own trembling cheeks from graduation day were still very much alive in me.
I just needed a little more time for them to fade away.
That's what I thought.
I missed him, but I wanted a bit more time to recover.
Until then, I would exchange words with Takaki… I could survive if I had that connection.

After winter came and was almost gone, I learned that he would be moving to Tanegashima.

6

I'm surprised that you'll be the one changing schools this

time.

I wasn't as calm as my words seemed on paper.

Since even I felt that way, Takaki couldn't have been, either, in writing that his father was being transferred to Tanegashima in Kagoshima Prefecture.

I'm pretty sure. Tanegashima…

Of course, I knew some facts about the island, like how it was where guns were first brought to Japan. I couldn't even begin to picture the place, though.

I hadn't even known that it was part of Kagoshima.

And where was that prefecture again?

On the southern tip of Kyushu.

Wasn't that all the way at the end of Japan?

The moment that thought came into my head, I finally realized how *far* it was.

> I know we've gotten used to changing schools a long time ago.
> Even so, Kagoshima is a bit far away.
> We won't be at a distance where we can just hop on a train if we wanted to meet. I guess that makes me feel kind of lonely.
> Takaki, please do take care of yourself.

As I wrote those words, I thought they weren't what I wanted to say at all.

Vexation started to kick around inside me.

I continued with my reply despite a grainy feeling that reminded me of the white noise on a TV screen.

Everything was blurry. The writing pad swayed in and out of focus.

Takaki is going to Kagoshima. Right.

Uh huh…

In my fuzzy mind, the words "Takaki is going to Kagoshima" kept flashing, but I couldn't figure out what they meant.

Then, an odd question echoed: *Why is he going so far?*

Why…

Why so far that we needed to take an airplane to see each other?

I…had assumed that he and I would always be connected, though at a distance.

Somehow I thought so, for no good reason.

Given where I was then, I should have known that it wasn't the case.

I am in Tochigi. He is in Tokyo.

We live so close to each other.

Why did I never think to meet him when he's so close by?

I haven't seen his face since he started junior high.

Why did I let my stupid fears put off something so important?

Those were just some of the thoughts that went through my head.

My brain was numb and my fingers were out of whack, but the letter that came from my pen was incredibly calm and detached. I didn't know why.

I didn't have a clue.

For the following few weeks, I was lost in a daze.

It was so cold that year that Tochigi still had snowstorms in late February.

In the morning, I would open the front door to find snow at my feet.

I'd brush a heap of it off the mailbox, head to the station, go through the ticket gates, and board the train.

Feeling the warmth of the heater by my feet in the gently rocking car, I would space out.

I liked to stick my temple against the chilly window glass. It would be as foggy as the scenery outside.

With my head also misty, I would still my breath at school, return home, open the mailbox to make sure it was empty, and then close it again.

That was how I spent those days. My teachers' lessons didn't reach me, and I couldn't care less what people around me were saying.

Somewhere in my subconscious, I imagined numbers counting down.

Takaki was somewhere I could reach if I just extended my hand, but soon I wouldn't be able to no matter how far I stretched.

I thought about calling him on the phone a couple of times, but my hand always stopped halfway and never allowed me to pick up the receiver.

I was still scared. How would I feel if his first words sounded cold? Plus...

If I called him...if we talked on the phone, I might accidentally blurt out something serious.

Even at that point, I was trying to avoid what was important.

Takaki didn't send a reply for a while.

In mid-February, I finally received a response. I read it in my room. Then, I stowed it away in a drawer, carefully locking it with a key.

The next morning, as I sat on the station bench and waited for my train, I began writing my response over my knees:

> Dear Takaki,
> I am so glad to hear that you're coming to visit on March 4th. It's already been a year since we've last met. I'm a little nervous.

In his letter, he had written something like this: "The distance between

Tochigi and Tanegashima is too great for us. When I move, we might not have the chance to meet for many years, maybe not even until we've grown up. I'd like to go see you one last time before then.

"So I was wondering if I could take the train to where you are, after school on March 4th. Since my parents will be out of town that day, I won't have to worry about coming home late. I hope you can come meet me at the station, even for just a little bit…"

I had read his letter all at once, taken a deep breath, and sighed.

Then I had reread it, over and over like always.

Ahh…

I thought to myself, once again, that the word "happy" didn't suffice.

Takaki—always said what I yearned to hear.

I knew I had been wishing for those words.

Yes… I think I had unconsciously hoped he would say them.

The only one who understood me had to go far away. It didn't make any sense.

But now there was something.

My body trembled when I thought about the day we would meet again.

I was finally going to see him…

I felt a mixture of anxiety and fear.

On my stationery, I wrote detailed directions for all the transfers from Shinjuku to Iwafune Station and drew little illustrations all around them.

For example, I drew long, long railroad tracks between Omiya and Oyama and even wrote "Far!" above it.

Tokyo and Tochigi were indeed so far we could cry.

I prayed—that the distance and time on the train ride wouldn't be too terrible for him.

That it would be as fun as possible.

And I told him:

Near my house, there's a large cherry tree. In spring, its petals probably fall at five centimeters per second too.

Bring spring with you, Takaki.

My clouded breath drifted away on the wind. As I sat on the chilly station bench and wrote my letter, a few scenes played back in my mind.

The day I transferred to that elementary school, which now felt so distant.

The words "You are going to be okay."

The day we held hands and fled from our classroom.

His hand, which felt bony but warm, holding mine.

And...

The day I whispered "five centimeters per second" under the fluttering cherry blossoms.

I still remember it as clear as day.

"Five centimeters per second" is special to me.

They were the first romantic words I ever uttered to a boy.

Yes...from that moment on...

I had wanted to hear his voice.

I had wanted to hold his hand.

I had wanted to feel his body heat. To gaze into his eyes. And...

Connecting as gently and naturally as the movement of a falling petal, as I had wished back at that moment, was no longer possible.

Abruptly parting and suddenly reuniting, in an unnatural manner, was the only option for us.

Now, and probably for good, I would never be able to tell him: *I hope we can see the cherry blossoms together again next year.*

But I loved Takaki Tohno.

Thank you for coming all the way to my station.

It's a long trip, so please be careful.

I'll be in the waiting area at seven in the evening.

5

The day of Takaki's visit finally arrived.

It was a weekday. I felt restless at school, but a thought occurred to me. When classes ended, I rushed home and went into the kitchen. I opened the refrigerator.

After getting out of school, Takaki wasn't stopping by at his house. He was heading straight to Shinjuku Station, and it was going to take him hours to get to Iwafune.

He was going to be hungry.

When I thought back on this moment many years later, I giggled out of embarrassment. I had acted like the stereotypical "girl in love" from an old soap opera.

The only lunchbox I found at home was a cute, small one for girls, and I wished we had a bigger and sturdier one.

In the lunchbox, I packed a rolled omelet, rice balls colored with pretty seasonings, and anything else I thought I could make by myself. I needed multiple tries to arrange the items neatly.

If Takaki and I had gone on to the same school, I might have packed him lunches like that all the time.

I wrapped the lunchbox in a cloth and carefully placed it in my bag so it wouldn't tilt to one side. For some reason this simple act made me feel as if my heart were about to burst.

The TV tried to warn me of a snowstorm before I left, but I didn't pay much attention.

It was after six o'clock and pretty dark outside.

Tiny snowflakes kept falling.

I crossed the front yard and headed to the station.

Walking down the straight farm road between rice paddies covered in thin layers of white snow, I felt anxious and harried. I started running.

I can meet Takaki soon.

I can meet Takaki now.

The old wooden station building came into view. He might have already arrived; I felt a large lump in the back of my throat.

I slid the door open by its aluminum latch and entered. The heat from the potbelly stove and the steam from the metal washtub above it gently warmed the room. I felt the stiffness in my frozen cheeks slowly melt away.

The waiting area was empty.

We had planned to meet at seven, but I had arrived much earlier.

I perched on a bench by the wall and placed my hands on my knees.

If I just waited, he would arrive in no time...

The sliding glass door to the platform would open...revealing Takaki.

What sort of expression was I supposed to wear?

What would he be like, after a whole year?

At that moment, my heart just might stop.

The old, worn-out stove whistled softly, and all of the windows were clouded white. It was as if I were in a box that had been cut off from the outside world.

Even the station attendant had withdrawn to the confines of his office. I silenced my breath so as not to disturb the quiet of the vacant waiting room.

I didn't mind waiting, at all.

Picturing Takaki on the train, drawing ever closer, made my chest quiver with excitement.

Maybe he was sitting on the window side in a booth and looking out at a wintry landscape rarely seen in Tokyo, and feeling the light vibrations of the train.

I imagined myself as Takaki and tried to feel the vibrations with him.

The wheels' steady rhythm as they roll over junctions came to life.

For a split second, I had this illusion that I was moving towards Takaki as he waited in place.

When seven drew near, I became fidgety, and my heart pounded loudly. I couldn't stop peeking at the round clock on the wall and the ticket gates' glass door.

I was glancing at the clock every fifteen seconds.

Time passed slowly, and my body began to sway.

The clock's hands pointed to several minutes past seven.

No one had come through the door to the platform—not a single person.

My fidgety joy turned into a different type of restlessness.

I tried peering at the platform through the foggy glass.

Just then, I realized that it had been a while since there had been any signs of incoming trains.

I promptly stood up, sped to the ticket window, and called to the station attendant. The reedy, aging gentleman answered me in a kind and measured tone.

"Right now, there's a very heavy snowstorm, with strong winds, y'see, and all the trains have stopped."

"What…"

"They're checking the tracks, and the trains in front have to go first. There'd be an accident otherwise, y'see. They're stopping and going, at stations and along the tracks, and moving slowly."

"Umm, do you know how late the seven o'clock train will be?"

"Hmm, when should it arrive… I can't really say. I'm not getting much information, either. Very sorry about that."

I weakly made my way back to the edge of the bench.

I watched my fingers clutch my knees.

Even after I had been told that the train was late, I couldn't keep my eyes off the clock.

My lips were pursed.

I stayed frozen in place.

Time slowed to a crawl.

I tried to stop glancing at the clock. I felt like not looking at it made the minutes go by faster.

The white noise of the stove and the water boiling above it was grating. That's how silent the room was.

When the wooden station creaked, or perhaps at some sound from beyond the ticket window, the back of my neck, and my ears, would twitch. Straining to get a better listen, just to learn that it was nothing, I would resume staring at the toes of my shoes.

Time crawled by.

In the span of about three hours, a few trains came and went.

Every time I heard one, I rose slightly from my seat to peer through the glass door, into the darkness of the raging snowstorm.

Tired faces floated through the ticket gates and the waiting room and disappeared outside on their journey home. My head stayed lifted for a while even after all of the passengers had left.

Finally convinced that Takaki hadn't been amongst them, I would settle back on the bench and hunch up again.

That happened a number of times.

I had never imagined that snow could suspend train service. In my year in Iwafune, I hadn't experienced anything like that.

Not personally, though perhaps I had been lucky.

So I was honestly shocked, and my emotions weren't catching up to the situation.

Snow had fallen and halted the trains.

Logically, I understood this.

But I couldn't believe it was actually happening.

Takaki couldn't come closer to me because of a snowstorm.

He was trapped inside a train stopped by the snow.

My heart ached just picturing it.

Snow fell at how many centimeters per second again?

I couldn't remember.

No doubt I would have been able to the day before, but most of my brain had completely shut down.

The outside world was dark and pure white, and droplets of water clouded the windows.

The fluorescent light on the ceiling must have been old because it was just a little dim.

A station waiting area that was like a square box—it felt like nothing else existed besides the world inside it.

And somewhere beyond the nothingness floated a long, narrow box that held Takaki.

It only takes three hours to get from Tokyo to Tochigi by train.

And I had thought *that* was far.

More than six hours had passed since he had begun his journey.

It was as if the distance had doubled. No, maybe it had more than doubled.

Right.

"This is what 'far' means," I muttered to myself.

Yet our distance now was nothing.

He was about to move even farther away…

I didn't know how to put my anguish into words.

I was really…very seriously anxious.

Time, only made up of the fizzing of the washtub on the stove, slowly crawled by.

Takaki isn't coming.

Takaki isn't coming.

I'm here alone.

And soon he'll go even farther away.

Something came rushing up from the bottom of my stomach. I clutched my fingers and clamped my mouth shut.

It felt as if a hand had reached into me to churn around my insides.

There was an uncomfortable feeling in the back of my throat, and I almost threw up.

At that moment...

I had an epiphany that ran through me like an electric current.

This is...
How he felt.

This was how Takaki felt when he heard I was moving to Tochigi.

Right. I got it.

The absurdity. The confusion.

A sinking, consuming frustration.

Anxiety in its wake.

I finally understood.

He, too, had felt miserable, lonely, and anxious.

Why hadn't I noticed when it was so obvious?

To me, Takaki was always—

Kind, reliable, unwavering... Someone I could count on to make me feel at ease.

I must have simply assumed that he was okay.

I was—

Filled with regret.

That final year. Right after our phone conversation.

Why hadn't I told him that I wanted to be with him more than anything, and that not a day went by where that wasn't true?

I felt that way from the bottom of my heart, so why hadn't I come out and said so?

If I had, he might have been spared his agony.

How could I blithely tell him "this is goodbye" on graduation day, when he probably feared that I was going away for good?

Five centimeters per second? What a happy-go-lucky, laid-back, and blissful notion.

During our phone conversation.

What had I been trying to get him to say?

Maybe I had wanted him to tell me I was going to be okay.

Not even realizing how he must have felt—had I been a hopeless baby?

I thought I heard a train arriving over the sound of the wind. I looked up.

My eyes were glued to the ticket gates.

I heard footsteps, I saw shadows; the glass door opened, and people came through.

An unfamiliar couple walking arm-in-arm—

They were the only ones who had gotten off the train.

I lowered my head almost as if I were embarrassed and desperate to make myself scarce.

My head was still hung when the couple passed me and exited the building.

Once the frigid blast from the glass door was cut off again, I let out a small sigh. Then, suddenly seized by an ominous thought, I tapped on the ticket window.

"Every train will eventually reach its destination," the attendant said. "But with the suspensions, it's conceivable to get stuck at a transferring station…"

He called the terminal to check for me.

They weren't certain, but it sounded like the suspensions in service began a bit after Takaki had left Oyama Station.

Which meant he must have hit a stop signal somewhere on the Ryomo Line, in the middle of nowhere.

Right?

I didn't know.

Maybe Takaki had tried to call my house from a station public phone to tell me that the trains were running late.

I considered calling my parents then rejected the idea.

No way.

I didn't want anyone else to get involved.

I didn't want to suffer more outside noise. Or trivial words.

I would wait.

Was Takaki coming or not?

4

Waiting.

It felt like time had stopped.

My head was heavy with fatigue.

Waiting for something uncertain and sensing the continuous passage of time numbed my nerves.

I was spacing out.

My brain was so numb that it almost felt good.

The delayed train.

The train that wouldn't come.

Somewhere in all of this I felt calm.

A train slowly approaching the end.

After all, Takaki was coming to say goodbye.

When his train arrived, everything would end. The train was an omen of the end of everything.

I didn't want his train to come.

I begged for time to stop.

Where did petals go after they fell on the ground?

They vanished.

They disappeared. They went someplace else.

I took some stationery out of my bag.

I placed the bag on my knees, put the stationery on top, and began to write a letter.

It was for Takaki.

Since my head was all muddled, I thought I might be able to write truly, unguardedly.

Paying no heed to order or structure, I put pen to paper. I wrote whatever came to mind.

I was going to give him the letter when he arrived.

How strange, that I was writing a letter premised on his arrival when I didn't know if he would actually make it.

His arrival would bring a final farewell.

Once he left, we wouldn't be meeting again. Possibly for many years. Perhaps not until we were adults.

I wrote everything I had wanted to tell him, to the best of my abilities.

I love you, Takaki.

I thought I could write that now. And I did.

The words "I love you" didn't describe what I felt for him at all.

Language was so vexing.

If only I could take the feelings from my body and show them to him: this is how much I feel for you.

But—

What was my love worth to him?

I didn't even know what I was worth myself.

I had curled into a crouch even as I addressed him.

The skin on my arms always stood up with fear.

I was as insignificant as a bug on the underside of a leaf. I knew this, and so did everyone else. I never stopped feeling that way.

The love of such a person was just laughable.

I did love him.

Despite all of that.

I love you...

I clung to those helpless words.

I pictured Takaki stuck inside a train, in the middle of a snowstorm.

The damp, heavy image of falling snow began to fill my heart.

It snowed.

Why couldn't it be cherry petals falling between us?

The Earth was round, and it was summer in the southern hemisphere.

Up until then, I had liked that image.

But now, I resented anyone who was basking in cherry petals on the other side of the world.

That was how I wanted him and me to be.

It was like a curse.

I hope we can see the cherry blossoms together again next year—

I had spoken those words without understanding a thing.

Thanks to that, it was never going to come true.

Takaki had been thrust into a snowstorm in his mistaken attempt to meet someone like me.

I was the one who was imprisoning him in snow.

Wasn't I, unable to sense anything good about myself, just like the Snow Witch of Narnia?

I was always making life hard for Takaki.

I was always hurting him...

3

Succumbing to exhaustion and the stove's heat, I finally fell asleep.

I had a dream. It was fragmentary. I couldn't tell if my eyes were open or closed.

Even when I felt a presence, I wondered if it wasn't just a fragment of my dream. What I had vaguely noticed was the navy-blue sleeve of a duffel coat.

I lifted my head.

Above the wall of that dark blue coat was Takaki's face.

It looked frozen with shock.

He was thinner and had a slightly longer face than I remembered.

My mind, still foggy and unable to process what was happening, transmitted emotion alone to my heart, awfully directly. For a time I sat inert, unable to think.

As Takaki stood there before me, I grabbed the hem of his coat, still gazing into his face. It was no hallucination. Tugged by me, Takaki took one small step closer.

The texture of his coat…

It gradually spread from my fingertips, and my face started feeling heavy. I could feel liquid rising just below the surface of my cheeks. Then it poured out of my eyes and drenched my face.

I looked down, still holding on to his coat. I could see droplets dripping on to the floor. It felt like something painful was stuck in the back of my throat.

I had not planned on crying. Yet my body, all on its own, made my chest convulse, sent out the liquid.

As I wept and clung to him, I suddenly sensed that some of the tears weren't my own. Amidst my sobbing I was nearly struck dumb.

Takaki was crying…

I was shocked.

The moment I noticed, my tears doubled. I didn't know I could cry so hard. Inside me some organ, similar to the heart, was plumbing an intense emotion and pumping it across my body.

"Intense emotion" is the only way I can describe it.

Neither joy, misery, nor pain, it coursed through me and came spilling out as tears.

Wanting to calm myself, I fixed my grip on his coat, swallowed my saliva, sniffled, and tried to catch my breath. The texture of his coat was unmistakable.

After I calmed down a bit…it hit me that he was actually here.

Takaki had come.

Just to meet me. Just for that purpose.

2

I felt bashful sitting next to him again after so long.

I poured tea from my thermos, into its lid, and handed it to Takaki. Receiving it with both hands, as if to warm himself, he took a sip.

"This is good," he said with genuine feeling for someone who usually spoke in a flat voice.

"Really? It's just roasted green tea."

"Roasted? This is my first time drinking it."

"No way. You've definitely had it before."

"You think so?"

"I know so."

I was glad that we were talking like we always had in the past.

Even though "the past" was really just one year ago.

Slightly offbeat, curious exchanges—right, we had been like this, always chatting about trivial stuff.

"Here you go. I can't guarantee it's any good, because I made it… but have some if you like."

"Thanks." Takaki sounded almost overcome with emotion. "I was starving."

He kindly took a rice ball that I had made. Well, it was already past eleven at night. He had been trapped in a train without food for seven hours.

Hoping he would say he liked it, I asked, "How is it?"

"It's the most delicious thing I've ever tasted," he replied, terribly earnestly, casting his eyes down a little.

"You're exaggerating." I bobbed my knees.

"It's true."

"You just think so because you're hungry."

"Is that it?"

"Definitely."

Tickled by our little back-and-forth, and happy, I nearly cried again. I had one of my own rice balls. I thought about how it was like a picnic with both of us eating the same thing, and couldn't suppress a bashful giggle.

After it subsided, I felt wistful.

"You're moving real soon," I murmured.

"Yeah, next week."

"To Kagoshima…"

"It's so far."

"Yeah…"

I still couldn't grasp exactly how far. But I was starting to understand what "distant" means.

"Though Tochigi is also pretty far," Takaki said. He must have been thinking the same thing.

"Right, you can't even go back home tonight."

He seemed startled by my comment, but I just laughed. What I was thinking: I didn't have to send him back home until the next day. Until then, I wanted to have him all to myself.

The station attendant lightly tapped on the window opposite the gates.

"We'll be closing up soon. There aren't any more trains tonight."

"Okay," Takaki said.

I wonder how the attendant saw us. I'm not quite sure, but his voice was really friendly. I found his kindness very comforting.

"There's a lot of snow out there, so please be careful," he said.

"Hey, let's go," I whispered to Takaki as if I were sharing a secret with him.

1

The wind had died down; the snow was just falling from the sky. It was cold outside, but not freezing.

On the seats and handlebars of the abandoned bicycles in the parking lot lay thick layers of white.

We walked side by side as we exited the old wooden station building.

The tiny falling flakes only twinkled where the streetlamps illuminated the darkness.

Our feet made a satisfying crunching sound on the fresh snow.

During the many hours I had spent at the station, it had snowed a great deal. No wonder the trains had stopped.

The thick blanket of snow had turned the roads pure white.

The boundary between the road and sidewalk was entirely buried, making the road appear much wider than it actually was.

The three-way intersection in front of the station looked more like some plaza.

Even though it was almost midnight, it didn't feel dark. The streetlamps shone circles of light on the snow at regular intervals.

The darkness seemed to glow thanks to the reflecting white ground.

It was the first time I had ever walked around in the dead of night—and after such heavy snowfall, too.

It was an exceptional sight.

Just like that, I started to run.

The road between the rice paddies was totally buried under snow as well. The fields were pure white, and if not for the telephone poles along the way, it would have been impossible to tell where the road ended and the fields began.

Far off in the darkness, a neat line of lattice towers stood out, black against a clouded sky.

Traveling down the dim road in a haze of snow, Takaki and I left a set of parallel footprints.

"Can you see that tree over there?" I asked as we walked.

"Is that the tree from your letter?"

"Yeah. The cherry tree."

We walked side by side along the road until we finally reached it.

It was a large, sturdy tree with winding branches that stretched out in every direction.

Its trunk was so thick that Takaki wouldn't have been able to wrap his arms all the way around it. Standing by its roots, we looked up at the branches that spread across the sky.

I was a bit moved.

I had longed to stand under that tree with Takaki. Ever since moving there.

The tree didn't have any leaves, of course, let alone flowers. It was completely bare.

Whenever I leaned against it, cradling one of Takaki's letters, I felt like I could hear his voice.

Yes... In my mind, he was like a cherry tree.

The light from some distant town reflected off the clouded sky, lightly fell onto the snow, and encased us in a frosty glow.

The cherry tree wore a pure-white veil.

Powdery snow fell.

"Hey..." I turned to Takaki. "Doesn't it look," I said, catching a snowflake in my hand, "just like snow?"

The wind blew, the snow danced, and there was a blizzard of flowers.

I was trying to summon an illusion with my remark: the light of spring surrounding us, the twisting trunk and branches bursting with pink clusters.

These are petals.

If they were indeed falling on the other side of the world—then this snow was the shadow cast by them.

The illusion I wove was instantly swept away by the frosty wind, and my mind returned to the dark, snowy night.

I must have been smiling, though.

"You're right," Takaki said softly, with a gentle look.

His reaction caught me off guard.

I could have sworn he'd reply with a question.

The pit of my stomach tightened at his straightforward answer.

That tightness took hold of me, and I stepped closer to him.

I was gazing into his eyes.

He was gazing into mine.

As if it were the most natural thing, though maybe a bit faster than five centimeters per second, we leaned towards each other.

I closed my eyes midway.

Then I—

0

I felt his lips against mine.

At that moment, I couldn't think about anything.

My consciousness was someplace else. It burned white as if it weren't my own. Instantaneous flashes ran through me like lightning. Dozens of images were burned into those flashes and vanished faster than I could perceive them. Sharp arrows, or what felt that way, rained down on me, cleansed my deepest impurities, and disappeared. When I was stripped of the excesses that had clung to me, the world vanished and I was all that remained.

I couldn't tell the difference between myself and the fragmented images flooding my head. For a few moments, I was Takaki. I grew excited, soared, and descended. I couldn't tell up from down. I was one pair of lips as well as the other. There was no distinction between them. I had discovered where abstract concepts like the heart, the soul, and eternity reside. I learned that Takaki and I were one, that we were two, that we could take different parts of each other and lock them safely in ourselves. The colors, heat, textures, and darkness that I felt then couldn't be put into words. It felt as if I had shared everything from my thirteen years with him, and I knew that Takaki thought the same.

We were one flawless existence. For just a single moment, we understood each other perfectly. Our individual selves disappeared and gave way to omnipotence. Complete fulfillment existed, for a moment. The moment almost lasted an eternity and nearly sucked me into its distortion. We were aware it was a miracle. Timings and circumstances miraculously lining up, the moment had visited us. The instant after we realized this…

I returned to just being me again, and felt his lips against mine.

The sorrow that overtook me was unbearable.

I sensed his body heat. I no longer knew how to handle it or where to take it. I was left with a feeling like regret, of having known until just now. The conviction that I would never know it again crept in through my fingertips, and my hands went limp.

I saw that life, impossibly large, lay before us, and that in its vague span of time, the perfect moment would never arrive again. It became all too clear to me that we could never be together. We had reached the finish line, and there was nowhere left to go.

Why this suddenly?

It was lonely and heartbreaking, and it hurt. I had hoped for something more gradual and natural, like the speed of a falling cherry blossom. But this was how we always ended up. A dooming miracle wasn't what I had wished for.

What should I do? What should I do?

The words whirled in my head. Confused, driven by the echoes of lost fulfillment, I threw my arms around Takaki's neck in despair. I pressed my cheek against his shoulder.

Over my warm winter clothes, with my entire body, I tried to feel all that was good and beautiful in him. Embracing him tightly, I stood still for a while.

His body heat dissolved my confusion and anxiety at long last, and thankfully, all that remained were joy and innocence.

A clump of snow thudded down from a branch.

From between the boughs covering the sky the snow fell ceaselessly.

He wrapped his arms around my back, and their strength was just intoxicating.

1

A tool shed sat in one corner of the field, and there we talked all night. We took off our coats, joined hands, and held each other, bundled in an old blanket we had found on a wooden shelf.

The entire time, I could feel his body heat.

We talked about all sorts of things.

For just a brief while during that long night, I fantasized about time stopping and everything staying just as it was… I wished he could whisk me away like he had that day at school.

But I knew it was impossible.

Not just because we were still kids… When our lips had touched, he, too, sensed what I did.

I didn't just believe this, I *knew* it.

We didn't breathe a single word about that moment the entire night. That flawless moment. An indescribable moment that would never come again. We didn't try to confirm that moment by describing it in words.

We could never be together after that.

Even without any transfers or moves, even if we could attend the same school, we just couldn't be together. In fact, being close would only remind us of what we had lost, and torment us.

Though I could foresee this…I still wished that time would stop.

Takaki had come to see me. That made me feel warm all over. He had come just to see someone like me, and here he was.

It felt nice to rest my cheek against his lean shoulder. Sinking into the dark, we didn't dream.

2

The next morning, I saw Takaki off at the station, where he would take the earliest train back to Tokyo.

We made the first footprints in the untouched snow on the platform. We held hands as we waited for his train.

Even with no one else around, we stood at the front end, as far away from the station building as possible.

The train arrived all too quickly.

With a loud hard sound it pulled into the station.

In just a couple of dozen seconds, the train would depart.

Takaki boarded the train and quickly turned to me. We looked at each other across the open doors.

"Um…Takaki…"

My hand hovered over the bag I was clutching to my chest. I was thinking about the letter I'd written at the station the day before.

I had written it to give to Takaki, to tell him all the things I never could.

But as I tried to fish out the envelope and hand it to him, my hand stopped halfway.

During our kiss—

What I can only call "the experience" that took place in me during it—

In light of that moment, I felt like my letter was inadequate. Its words said nothing and would only devalue the miracle.

Language was just noise compared to the experience's pureness.

The intense emotion of that moment outstripped what I had written in my letter, which was fated to become a degraded record.

That moment can never be put into words.

The words "I love you" seemed practically hollow. My chest tightened at the thought of him, I longed to be with him so badly I could die, while the words "I love you" didn't even sound real.

Still, there was one thing I knew I had to say to him no matter what.

The moment I tried, I nearly started crying.

Raising my face—as though buoyed by my overflowing feelings—I declared, "You're going to be okay from now on, Takaki! I just know it!"

That was the only thing I absolutely needed to say.

The words I had wanted to hear from someone.

I spoke them to my other self, who stood there, and to myself. Thanks to Takaki visiting me despite the snow, there had been a change in me.

I don't know how best to describe it, but it was a definite transformation. Seeing Takaki's face that night at the station had cleared away my constant, cowering fear of life.

According to the vocabulary of the grownup I am today: I had been blessed.

Takaki had come to bless me.

And I wanted to do the same for him.

Having the strength to tell people that they're going to be okay—that really *is* important.

Or so I believe, long afterwards, as an adult.

A whistle sounded, at quite a distance, and with a compressing whoosh the doors began to shut.

"Thank you," Takaki said at almost the same moment that they did.

The train started to glide out of the station.

Bringing his face close to the doors, he called out, "Take care, Akari!"

He pressed his hand against the glass.

"I'll write letters! And call!" he shouted.

Our positions were no longer in sync.

He seemed to get smaller and smaller as the train steadily accelerated.

A whistle tore the air again, and a bird flapped its wings and took off from some branch.

In no time at all, the train had gained speed and vanished. I felt a sudden pang of loss.

Motionless, I stared into the direction that the train had gone.

A railway signal flashed red.

I looked up to find wisps of low clouds floating in the blue morning sky. Fresh snow unspoiled by footprints coated the front end of the platform.

All of it seemed like a scenic description meant to indicate that Takaki was gone.

However.

I stood there confident that I could take on life.

No matter how far he went, he was with me.

He, at least, will always understand me perfectly. I have such a person—that thought alone was reassuring, and I could make it, even if I was on my own there.

Oh, what to do with me...

While I felt a deep sense of loss, I was strangely fulfilled.

So I told myself:

We'll meet again someday, though it won't be soon, and I'll try to be a stronger person by then.

But we would never meet again.

Chapter Two
Cosmonaut

15

Akari and I stopped writing to each other many years ago.

14

I had finished my first year of junior high. The morning after the end-of-term ceremony, I flew from Haneda to Kagoshima Airport.

Even though it was my first time flying alone, I didn't run into any problems checking in and boarding the plane. My parents had moved to Tanegashima earlier than planned. Since they had told me to at least show up to my last end-of-term ceremony in Tokyo, I ended up following them to the island by myself.

After one hour and fifty minutes of sitting still in an economy seat, I arrived in Kagoshima. I didn't feel uneasy or really anything at all.

As strange as it may sound, it comforted me to know that there wouldn't be any stopovers once the plane had taken off.

I found a shuttle bus at the airport and got on.

I dozed off for a bit and woke up in Kagoshima City. When I looked out the window, I saw trams running parallel to each other, moving along the wires above the center of the wide road.

I got off the bus in front of Kagoshima City Hall and followed my photocopy of a map to the harbor. Due to the broadness of the road and the lack of high-rise buildings, it felt like the sky was incredibly vast. When I saw the palm trees that lined the road, it really hit home that I had come to southern Japan.

When I boarded the express ferry to Tanegashima, I could see a large, brown, rocky mountain on the other side of the large bay. It looked like it was blocking the exit to the sea. When I researched the mountain later, I found out that it was the famous Sakurajima, "Cherry Blossom Island."

I somberly continued my journey.

My father met me at Nishinoomote Harbor, and then he drove for about an hour towards the town of Minamitane.

We took the national highway all the way down the coast to Minamitane. When I opened my window, I could smell the ocean.

To this day, I still remember that fresh, intoxicating scent.

The town broke off into a pale-green field that extended across the land between the previous town and the next.

Further beyond the fields stood a pristine, dark-green mountain. Then, the mountain dropped off into the ever-shimmering sea.

This place seemed nothing like Yamano in Nagano Prefecture, a place where I used to live when I was younger. Maybe it had something to do with the different vegetation.

Yeah, I guess I was just impressed—I didn't think beautiful places like it still existed in Japan.

My family and I had moved into a detached house made of wood. It had been a while since we lived in an actual house.

Despite the building's old age, its interior decorations were relatively charming, and it had even been cleaned before our move. The rather thick, dark-brown wooden beams that ran across the ceiling gave the house a fairly luxurious feel. More than anything, it really was quite big.

My father said that living in a house might feel nice after all those years we had spent in apartments. It certainly was refreshing.

Not bad at all.

I went out into the garden and gazed off into the remarkably vast, deep-blue sky.

The sky in Kagoshima City had felt massive enough already, but in the garden it was almost a whole size larger.

It felt like my head hadn't caught up with reality.

The train in the snow still lingered in me. The snowflakes pelting against the window, the overpowering heater, the anxiety—I felt these things constantly.

The two realities were so different that it made my head spin.

I thought back to the view of the island I had in my father's car.

I remembered learning about windbreaks and sugarcane fields in school, but it was my first time seeing them in real life.

I had come to a rural island.

This place will do for now.
I'm just going to leave again anyway.

13

In April, I transferred to Minamitane Junior High School.

I was somewhat relieved to hear that I would be wearing the same standard, black uniform that I had worn at my last school.

After changing schools so many times, I was already a veteran. I perfectly understood how a transfer student should behave.

I think it's partly because Akari had provided an example.

After watching her, my vague grasp of what it meant to be a transfer student had turned into a completely conscious understanding.

While I'm sure everyone has similar realizations whether it's in college, at a job, or somewhere else down the line, gaining that knowledge at the young age of fourteen had given me an enormous advantage. You could even call it my weapon. This is what I had learned:

Do not fear attracting attention.

Do not enjoy attention too much.

Do not stand out, but also do not hush your breath. You must subtly show others that you mean them no harm.

The hosts are also afraid.

You must understand that.

For a short time—for a period of about one month, or a month and a half—new transfers have *celebrity status*.

What you do while you have that status determines victory or defeat. You should learn all of your classmates' names because people like to feel remembered by a celebrity. Their positive impression of you will be your key to making friends.

In any case, never act like you do not fit in.

Children are sensitive to that and will reject you on sight.

All fourteen-year-olds think they are adults, but they are just kids.

"Childish" is the only way to describe their reaction to outsiders. It was something I already knew to be painfully true.

In terms of the above guidelines, I don't think I received many compliments on my class greeting when I first transferred to junior high, but I don't think I was complained about, either.

"I've gotten used to changing schools for my dad's job...but I still haven't gotten used to this island. It's nice to meet you."

I probably couldn't hide how much I hated that I had to be there.

Kanae Sumida was in my class, but I didn't specifically notice her then. Nor did I notice her for a while after that.

It has been years since I graduated junior high and high school.

I'm writing this because I can't forget what happened back then. I'm going to write about myself...and then about Kanae, whom I doubt I will ever meet again.

Now that I think about it, I'm almost certain that the first time she and I talked was about a week after I transferred in.

I had pretty much figured out who was friends with who and which of the kids were the movers and shakers.

In that sense, I found a girl who had no label.

I don't really remember what we talked about. I assume this means our conversation didn't strike a chord in either of us.

If I am remembering correctly, I think she was kind enough to show me to my next class.

That's right, she came right up to my desk and told me how to get there. I think she said, "Next is science," or something like that.

I was a bit surprised how Kanae Sumida, whom I had never spoken to before, randomly came to tell me that, but I didn't think much of it. I just figured that she was one of the nice girls.

We probably walked together through the hallway that led to the corner of the second floor, where a science room with black countertops let in so much sunlight that it made you drowsy.

Because of the strong winds on the island, clouds of sand swept in from the grounds. It was always dusty in the building no matter how often it was cleaned.

Since there were barely any students, I passed several empty classrooms when I walked those sandy hallways.

You never found sandy hallways or empty classrooms at a junior high in Tokyo. These details made me feel as if I had traveled to an unfamiliar land.

Light from the bare southern windows poured into the deserted classrooms, reflected off the white ceilings and floors, and shone bright into the hallway.

That strong, penetrating light has been burned into my mind as a symbol of my life as a student on Tanegashima.

Kanae was probably watching as I took in that view with squinting eyes.

At the time, I didn't notice these things. I was oblivious.

I didn't notice because my surroundings were too new to me and I was nervous about fitting in, and also because...Akari was too important to me.

I was just staring at the grounds through a window in an empty classroom when I spotted a newly painted soccer goal lying on the ground.

I had been a member of the soccer club at my old school but hadn't rejoined.

I had lost all interest in sports. Something had changed.

12

Every day I had off from school, I toured the island on my bicycle.

On the first Sunday after I transferred, I went straight to the only bookstore in Minamitane and bought a guidebook on Tanegashima. It was the kind that had a map in it listing the island's tourist attractions.

Using the book as my guide, I traveled to all of the picturesque spots. I was way too restless to stay in one place.

When I started junior high, my aunt in Nagano bought me a mountain bike, which I ended up using quite a lot.

I called it a "mountain bike," but it wasn't actually meant to climb mountains. It was just an ordinary bike from a hardware store. In fact, its manual even contained the warning "Do not ride through the dirt." That being said, it was equipped with slick tires and rode just fine if you pedaled hard enough.

Tanegashima is the fifth largest offshore island in Japan, so traveling its entirety is much easier said than done.

Minamitane was on the southern tip, and I worked my way north, visiting a tourist spot or two every weekend.

Tanegashima is a thin and narrow island that stretches nearly forty miles from north to south.

Riding my bike from Minamitane to Nishinoomote, a city up

north, would be tough. Not impossible, but counting backwards I figured that it would probably be too dark to see on the way home.

Despite that, I spent many weekends sleeping at the Urata Beach Resort campgrounds, on the northern tip of the island, before going back to circling the island the next day.

Tanegashima Space Center was the place I went to first.

When I pedaled a few miles along the river and up a straight uphill road, I was already standing on NASDA grounds (JAXA was still called NASDA back then).

My bicycle chain creaked all the way up the slope. When I finally reached the top, the horizon expanded beneath me.

A faded lawn, which could have been a golf course or a meadow, spread there.

An asphalt road ran straight through its center.

Beyond that lay the ocean.

Tanegashima's sea seemed to be riddled with craggy rocks.

Striped, light-brown Miocene sandstone reminiscent of Mars' surface jutted colossally out of the water everywhere.

Centuries of violent erosion had worn away the shore, revealing the deep red of the soil—exposing the island's true colors which had been hidden under a blanket of green.

Far beyond the colossal red stones, a cape protruded into the sea. At its tip were two horn-shaped steel towers and a square white building.

That was the launch site.

I laid my bike on its side and stood in the middle of the road. Lifting my eyes to the expansive, if somewhat overcast sky, I imagined a soaring rocket.

Which way was it flying, though, and how?

I couldn't really picture it.

Despite having seen news footages of a rocket launch plenty of times, somehow I couldn't imagine it realistically.

Maybe the sky was just too vast.

The sea looked so wide from the hilltop that I felt like I could perceive the Earth's roundness by staring at the horizon. This wasn't Tokyo's narrow but directive sky.

In the two years I spent on the island as a junior high student, I became obsessed with gazing at the sea.

Whenever I had time to kill, I would climb the Kamori Summit Observation Deck. I would strain my eyes to see the blur in the distance that was Yakushima Island.

When I got tired of that view, I would go to the park at Cape Kadokura and take in the salty smell of the tide. Centuries ago, a Portuguese ship carrying what would become Japan's first muskets had drifted to that shore. I would stay there for hours and watch spots of clouds lightly covering the blue sky turn uneven shades of red.

I also often visited Shimama Port.

It was the perfect place to watch a sunset. You could even go fishing. The sun would begin to dip while I amused myself watching merchant ships get unloaded.

At the sight of the sun blazing like coal and sinking into the sea, I would feel mesmerized as if the apocalypse had come.

Thus I made many places on the island my own.

If I rode my bike early in the morning, I could smell the morning dew.

When that morning dew evaporated in the hot southern sun, I could smell the grass and the leaves.

If I rode my bike on the national highway along the coast, I could smell the sea.

When I could smell the rain, there would be a sudden downpour in the evening.

Burning rubber on the asphalt, I smelled all kinds of voluminous aromas come and go. Through those shifts, I confirmed that I was moving.

I had to keep going.

I would have gone crazy otherwise.

That was truly an island of various aromas.

The colors and atmosphere were so intense that they almost made me dizzy.

I sent Akari a letter describing my new life on the island.

I wrote that I felt oddly relieved that the student body was much smaller than in Tokyo, with only two classes per grade.

I said that Tanegashima surprised me; it was far more beautiful than I had expected.

Then I went on about the island.

About the vivid contrast between the red soil, the dark green mountains, and the fields that were a lighter green.

About the starry sky I saw from Hoshihara, or "Starry Field," Beach after sneaking out of my house in the middle of the night.

The ancients must have looked up at the night sky and given Hoshihara its name. When I stood on that beach, I had an unobstructed 180-degree view of the endless sky and the sea. If the waves ever subsided, I might even see the stars reflected in the sea...

Akari's letters had changed a bit ever since that wintry day.

Her previous letters' melancholy nuance, which felt dressed up in fake cheer, now seemed to be fading. For the most part, she seemed to be doing well.

After two quiet and fulfilling years, I graduated from junior high and enrolled at a high school ten miles away in Nakatane.

11

Deep down, I think I knew that my correspondence with Akari wasn't going to last.

My letters to her were always pages long, and her replies were just as extensive. I wrote about both the important and trivial things that were going on in my life. An almost competitive sense of urgency took over and forced me to line up hundreds of words. I imagine that Akari felt the same way.

We were trying desperately to stay in touch.

We needed to believe that we were connected through a special circuit—so we labored over our letters.

But we couldn't go on tormenting ourselves like that forever.

Burying my white stationery in words, I always felt the urge to claw at my desk in frustration. It was as if I had locked my greatest treasure in a safe that I was now unable to open.

The experience we had shared on that snowy night.

Akari didn't write a single word about it in her letters. She never even vaguely referenced it. I fully understood how she felt.

Because I felt the same way. I didn't write one word about it, either.

We didn't plan for it to turn out that way. It was all we could do.

That moment...

What had happened under the cherry tree was too ideal.

That is all I can say.

No metaphor can describe it.

On that day, in that place, there had been a *perfect moment*.

A moment of absolute purity.

It had everything.

Nothing more perfect could possibly exist.

That moment bound perfection to a certain place. We couldn't bring it anywhere else.

It was a moment that could never be put into words.

Doing so would slice it up and preserve it...like some sort of specimen on display.

We couldn't do that to the experience that had changed us forever.

Forcing a description on the indescribable would only tarnish and degrade its original brilliance.

Which was why...

After that experience, I never told Akari that my letter to her had been swept away in a gust of wind on a platform along the way.

On the last day we met, since we were going to be torn apart, I had prepared a letter to tell Akari how I felt. I wanted to express in writing everything I couldn't say in person. In the end, the wind stole that letter, whisking it off somewhere.

But I'm glad about it.

Linguistic expression is so inaccurate and crude.

Words can't reproduce anything.

I had seen the universe.

To put it in metaphorical terms, the letter I wrote before that experience is the ancients' belief that elephants carry Earth on a plate. No way I could hand her something so inaccurate as a representation of my feelings.

I was genuinely shocked by the frightening inaccuracy of the tool we call language.

Even though I knew they could never express my feelings, words were all I could send her.

I could only try to feel her through her words, on the other side of the stationery.

Akari's letters couldn't contain the truths witnessed on that fateful day either, but I sought the remnants of that overpowering experience in our correspondence. I tried to stop seeking it but couldn't help myself.

Not finding it wore me out eventually.

For the first few years in Tanegashima, part of my daily routine was to check the mailbox on the way to and from school.

No, it was more of an unbreakable habit than a routine.

I waited for her letters as if I were clinging to them.

Whenever I found a letter from her in my mailbox, a sort of helplessness also snuck into my joy.

Truly, that moment...

No matter how far I reached, I couldn't retrieve what I had so clearly held in my hands.

I tried to put it into words more times than I could count.

Yet whenever I went to write it down, it always turned into something else.

I felt helpless...

And I'm sure Akari did, too.

If she wrote one more word, she would enter uncharted territory. After much hesitation, as if suddenly falling silent, she would halt her pen. I could sense that at least, and sensed it profoundly.

I knew that feeling well. The limitations of words. Like being at the edge of a cliff, unable to move forward. Even if you tried, your mouth would move in vain. Like a stereo with muted speakers. The CD turns. The music plays. But no sound is coming out...

Then, one day, we gave up on trying to share that special feeling in our letters.

Just like that, they turned into a mere report of events, losing all of their depth and profundity. We were merely exchanging words on paper.

And then our correspondence came to an end.

When it became clear that I would no longer be sending or receiving any letters, I felt oddly relieved.

After that ephemeral relief passed, and the deep colors of reality painted over Akari's lingering presence in me, what silently crept in was a hollow but refreshing feeling—that I may never wish to be understood again.

10

When I started living on the island, one of the things that surprised me was that all of the high school kids rode scooters and motorcycles to school like it was nothing.

When I passed by the library, I often saw a petite motorcycle in the parking lot facing the national highway. A girl in school uniform, and sporting an open-faced white helmet, would come out of the library, straddle her motorcycle, give the ground a practiced kick, and speed away.

The school had given her permission to come by motorcycle, of course.

Being from mainland Japan, I found the idea of motorbiking to school really odd. To be honest, I still find it odd.

While Tanegashima was quite large, there wasn't a single railroad on the island. Buses were also in short supply. Traveling by motorcycle might be convenient, but bicycles also seemed like an option.

Or so I had thought.

When I started cycling from Minamitane to my high school in Nakatane, however, I learned that a motorcycle was an absolute necessity. It was essential for survival.

When I first started high school, I had gone by bike.

It was exactly ten miles from my house to the school. I measured it out with a ruler and map.

Seems like a reasonable distance for some daily exercise. People are always saying how the terrain here is flat. It should be a piece of cake.

I was pretty certain.

But after a couple of brutal weeks on my bike, I realized that I had made a terrible mistake.

Who the hell said Tanegashima was flat?!

To put it simply, people only thought the island was flat because it didn't rise to a mile above sea level like Yakushima. While it's only common sense, an island is a landform that sticks out of the ocean. So it naturally has more bumps and abrupt slopes than the mainland's plains.

I didn't mind riding uphill when I was sightseeing. However, once those uphill treks became a part of my daily routine, my body and soul felt as heavy as lead.

Right by the area between Minamitane and Nakatane was a depression as deep as a valley. Although a fantastic rustic landscape expanded beneath me on either side, it meant tackling a sharp, steep hill whenever I left or went home.

If I hustled to make it in time for the morning bell, my heart and lungs felt like they might collapse from the climb.

If I ever went full speed downhill without hitting the breaks, I would definitely lose control and either fall or crash into something.

And that wasn't all.

Strong winds from the sea slammed the island all throughout the year. Fighting the oncoming winds wore me down to the core.

Even on the national highway, there were no streetlamps or anything of the sort. Since there wasn't a single house outside of town, the area became pitch black in the early hours of the night.

I'm not exaggerating when I say pitch black. It got so dark that I couldn't tell where the road ended or began. The headlights on my bicycle were virtually useless.

The worst part was that it rained in that darkness. Evening showers came like clockwork as if someone were being spiteful.

So I finally decided to call it quits. I crammed all night, passed the written exam for my motorcycle license, and asked my parents to buy me the Honda Super Cub, which was recommended by my school.

My Cub was a small 50 cc motorcycle, a scooter. I like Cubs. They have compartments to store your things and a transmission that rapidly zips you uphill. Mine even had plastic fairings by the footpegs to deflect the wind. My Cub was sturdy and practical.

Which reminds me… Kanae had recommended from the outset that I buy a Cub.

I had too much confidence in my physical strength to listen to her.

"I don't need a Cub," I had told her proudly. "I can just use my bicycle."

But my attitude completely flipped soon afterwards.

The first morning I motorbiked to school, I ran into her in the parking lot. She had also come to school on a Cub.

"I told you," she said.

I "rediscovered" Kanae Sumida at the beginning of high school, before summer, when I was still riding my bicycle to school.

I pedaled down the straight road from Nakatane High south to Nakayama Beach.

The town broke off into nothing but empty fields on either side. I sped past a coin-operated rice polisher, rode up and down the low hills in the woods, and saw decayed motorboats lining the streets. When I pressed on, the surrounding woods cut off all at once and a beach suddenly came into view.

There was a parking lot that faced a dock, which had concrete revetments. But I never saw any boats parked at the dock. No one ever used it, so no one was ever there.

To the right of the harbor was a pure-white beach that curved far into the distance. I scooped up the tiny grains of sand and watched them glitter in my hands.

The ocean was vast, its color was dark, and the shrinking undulations in the distance turned into foamy white waves, which at times created small tubes that rolled onto shore.

I never grew tired of gazing at that view.

But I hadn't come to look at the sea. I picked up a heavy white stone from a corner of the parking lot, placed it in the sand, and sat on it to smoke a cigarette. No one ever came by.

Back then, there weren't any weird Taspo cards that served as your ID at cigarette vending machines. It was a blissful era where you could buy as much vending-machine tobacco as you liked. I wonder how kids who want to smoke in high school are doing these days.

I vacantly stared out at the ocean and fiddled with the sea bindweeds by my feet. Way out in the distance, I could see a bodyboarder paddling out to the open sea.

Well, this is rare, I thought. *Swimming is prohibited at this beach.*

While no one was around and it was a convenient place to practice, I wondered if the bodyboarder would be okay.

The yellowish wetsuit was easy to spot in the water. The bodyboarder looked kind of small and was probably a girl. She fought wholeheartedly against the waves, clung to her board when they threw her back to shore, and repeated the cycle. She seemed too new at the sport to call her skills good or bad.

Yet, for some reason, I found her moving.

She seemed desperate, as if her goal was to paddle and fight the waves rather than ride them.

As I watched her keep at it, a strange sense of urgency welled up in me.

I felt like I was slacking off when I should be fighting like her.

I put my cigarettes and portable ashtray in my pocket and, a cold rock still below my butt, continued to gaze at the petite bodyboarder. Then it hit me: *Isn't that Kanae?*

I stared at the girl for a few minutes. It was definitely Kanae Sumida.

She, too, had gone from Minamitane Junior High to Nakatane High. We were in the same grade but had no classes together. There were only two high schools near Minamitane, so it wasn't odd that we had ended up at the same one.

Huh, I didn't know Kanae surfs.

Although this was news to me, I wasn't surprised.

She was an athletic girl with the quintessential "islander" vibe, and it only seemed fitting that she was into water sports.

For a while, I watched absentmindedly as she tried to stand on her board then almost immediately fall off. Seeming to call it quits, she started back towards the beach. When it was shallow enough for her to walk, she began parting the water with her shins above the sandy floor, her bodyboard following behind by the strap attached to her leg.

That was when she finally noticed me and flinched.

"Hey," I said, figuring that it would be more natural to talk than stay silent. I didn't know why she looked like she had seen a ghost. She seemed mortified, as if I had caught her doing something embarrassing.

"Tohno…" she said, stopping where she stood. She started towards me, then stopped again several feet away. She was still a little out of breath.

"What? Why did you come here?" she asked in between rough breaths.

"I just kind of stumbled upon this place…" That was really the only reason. "I didn't know you surfed."

"Well, um…" Kanae interlaced her fingers in front of her. She seemed uncomfortable. I guess I had shown up at an awkward time.

With apparent determination, she briskly walked up to me, stood next to me, and finally sat down in the sand.

"I can't call myself a surfer yet. I've only just started," she said. It sounded like she was facing down.

She might have sat next to me to keep me from looking at her skin-tight wetsuit. My eyes politely turned to the white edges of the waves rolling to shore. The image of Kanae's unexpectedly slender legs stayed with me for a while, though.

"Isn't the water still freezing? It's really impressive that you come here straight from school to practice."

"Thanks…"

"Do you practice every day?"

"Not every day. And I'm not impressive at all."

I genuinely thought that her efforts were admirable, but didn't argue the point. She seemed upset with herself. I empathized with that feeling, and she might not appreciate lame attempts to cheer her up.

"Do you often come to this beach, Tohno?"

"Not really. I've only been here two or three times before."

"You don't say. I guess you're just as strange as I thought…"

"Me? Why?"

"People don't usually come here alone to watch the sea."

"I guess I see your point."

"Yeah, it's a little strange."

Maybe she was right. People don't tend to randomly go to the beach and space out in real life.

Even so, hearing a local girl call me "strange" made me a little self-conscious. I was pretty detached and didn't care how people viewed me, but I felt alienated at the same time. It wasn't very pleasant.

"Bodyboarding is beautiful," I said. I wasn't trying to flatter her, I was just being honest.

She turned my way. "Yeah? You really think so?"

"Definitely. Something about it is really stirring. It must feel nice to ride the waves, but even better to paddle out towards the glimmering sea."

"Oh, I feel the same. Heading out to the ocean is the best."

"What's it like?"

"Umm, it kind of feels like 'I got this!' or 'Today's the day!' or something… I, uhh, can't describe it all that well, but it's like 'Here it comes!' and 'Almost there…'"

"The tension of going to capture that moment."

"Right, it's like that." Kanae's eyes were wide with surprise. "How do you come up with that stuff so quickly?"

"I don't really."

"I wish you'd always talk this much."

"I talk all the time."

"I don't know… I have this image of you, Tohno. Even with your friends, I feel like you stop yourself mid-sentence when you have more to say."

"I guess… Hey, if it's okay with you, I'd like to watch you surf some more," I changed the subject.

"No way!" Kanae shot me down. She practically recoiled.

"Why not?"

"Because I stink at it."

"No, you don't."

"I'm different from you, Tohno."

"In what way?"

"In a lot of ways. It's a tangled mess. Not easy to explain."

"If you say so…"

We weren't different. It was just that when the lines became crossed, I couldn't accept it. I couldn't admit it.

When Kanae was ready to leave the beach, I invited her to visit a convenience store with me.

"Wha… Are you sure?" she asked, not making any sense. Since I'd invited her, I was quite sure.

Kanae told me to wait as she "changed real quick," then disappeared into the thick brush of the coastal woods.

I stood there momentarily puzzled when a thought crossed my mind: *How did Kanae get here? It'd be a pretty tough walk. Maybe by car?*

Before long, pulling a Cub up beside her, she emerged from the dense thicket. She had changed into her school uniform and thrown a bath towel over her shoulder.

I was more amazed than surprised that she could change outdoors.

Leave it to the island girl. Tokyo girls could never even imagine doing such a thing.

Kanae's natural fearlessness dazzled me.

With me on my bike and her on her Cub, we headed to a nearby Ai Shop. That's a Kagoshima convenience store chain, and it was the only establishment resembling a modern store along the road from Nakayama Beach to Minamitane. I like convenience stores, though. Cheap, laid-back, and relaxing.

Since I pedaled at full speed and Kanae went slow, our paces almost matched. I was completely out of breath by the time we arrived.

We bought drinks and made small talk on a faded bench outside the store. We talked about our new classes, our teachers, that kind of stuff.

Kanae urged that I get a motorcycle. Still set on my bicycle at that point, I pretended I didn't need a Cub, but deep down…I started having second thoughts.

What bothered me more, though, was Kanae's observation back at the beach.

That I stopped talking when I seemed to have more to say.

I felt like she'd gotten me where it hurts.

Maybe I *was* weirdly self-conscious. Maybe my attitude did leave such an impression.

I was blown away. Kanae, a girl who didn't stand out much at school or know me very well, had hit the nail on the head.

If she began to occupy a special place in my heart, then that might have been why.

Since that day, Kanae and I grew closer.

We would wave or exchange looks every time we encountered each other in the hallway. When our other friends weren't there, we would stand around and chat.

On really rare occasions, when we got out of school at the same time, we also rode home together on our Cubs. And... Well, that was about the extent of our friendship.

Kanae always looked a little nervous when she was talking to me.

While she seemed more charming to me when she was chatting cheerfully with her classmates, around me she was a bit tense. But I knew she didn't hate me. She didn't hate me at all.

What I'm trying to say—and this might sound pretentious—is that she was crushing on me, maybe.

The joy in her face when she saw me said as much.

I made sure not to react in any way. In other words, I pretended not to notice and totally put off dealing with it.

But I did honestly like her as a person. I loved her energy. Her vibes always put me at ease.

It had been some time since I'd felt that way.

In any case, it was nice having a friend of the opposite sex I could talk to. I felt myself unwinding every time we met up.

In fact, being around her showed me just how tense I'd been.

Whenever I was with Kanae, I felt a little more comfortable.

My father's job was going well and the transfers seemed to be over. It seemed like he was going to work in Tanegashima until he retired.

Whether I liked it or not, my roots began sinking into the ground. I could feel it.

I was starting to get stuck.

Keep transferring for too long, and you get into the habit of thinking that all places are temporary. You never let yourself feel at home.

Even on the island I had taken that stance. Just like I always had. Just like I had whenever I moved.

But my basic worldview was beginning to fray.

"I want to go somewhere," I would blurt out when I was alone, to my own astonishment.

Did that just come from me, the kid who was raised as a nomad? Do I really want that?

Changing residences—or moving—had always been something that was forced on me, not what I was supposed to want. Hadn't I always accepted it with solemn resignation, knowing that my only option was to knock down everything I had built up and to start again from scratch?

Why did I want to leave?

Maybe I felt frustrated.

At myself, for gradually accepting the island as my home.

I mulled over this for quite a long time. I thought about my vague desires.

"I want to go somewhere" probably contained a nuance of "I want to go home."

But where was home? I didn't have a hometown. I never felt a special attachment to any place because I never put down roots.

Where did I want to return?

Had I left anything behind?

For the first time in a while, I thought about Akari. But that neighborhood that was no longer hers couldn't be it.

Then I had the dream.

9

The heavens were inconsistent. A dull, enchanting light glimmered in a dark sky clearly not of this world. In the black-blue zenith floated a nebula, a faded burgundy and faint-blue pattern like dissolving paint.

Towards the pattern, the wind blew thick white clouds that had a depth. Behind them stars sprinkled in the sky played peek-a-boo. Some of them loomed large and carved a blurry cross of light into the celestial canvas. Thin contrails spiraled up.

Just below the firmament, two birds crossed over each other and flew far into the distance.

Starting from the zenith, my eyes traced the downward flow of the nebula against the indigo background.

The color faded as it approached the horizon, transitioning from indigo to dark blue, from blue to the faint green of a coral lagoon.

Light leaked in from below the horizon.

Very slowly, but surely.

That faint green was gradually eroding the deep night. The transformation seemed quite gentle—a kind light seeping into a kind darkness.

It looked like I could squeeze the passing clouds if I reached out to touch them.

I could hear the wind.

The undergrowth covering an entire hill swayed in waves.

Right, I was on a hill.

A view of the widest sky, and the farthest horizon.

Maybe it was the center of the universe. Nothing here was manmade.

Yet everything was perfect.

Two figures drew near, walking on the soft grass.

They climbed the hill.

I was one of them.

The other was a girl.

Rustling footsteps in the grass.

We climbed to a certain height, then stopped.

She sat on the grass.

A white flower bloomed.

What looked like a dragonfly fluttered its wings and flew away.

The girl and I were enveloped in a clear, green light.

We stared up at the sky from the hill.

The distant light-green sky.

The wind flowed endlessly through the grass, the trees, the flowers, and the girl's hair.

We watched.

A giant sphere climbed the horizon and revealed its entire dark-blue form.

It was a massive planet leagues larger than the Earth's moon. I could even feel its gravitational pull dragging me in. It couldn't actually be a moon.

This was a binary planet, I realized. The girl and I were standing on a planet that circled another, as if holding hands. We watched the fated partner unveil itself in the gentle light of dawn.

Then—the sun appeared.

A white light, born just below the blue planet. The tiniest glimpse peeking out from below the horizon transmuted the atmosphere. An intense, devastating force was released upon a once gentle world.

It overwhelmed the blue planet and chased the stars back into the heavens.

The hues of the night receded from the sky.

I could see light pouring forth in every direction.

The sun silently ascended.

As it rose higher, its rays struck the ground, and our shadows darted behind us.

The vegetation basked in the glow, and their colors deepened.

The sunlight pierced the thin, low-lying clouds from below, throwing their shadows into the heavens.

An immaculate halo surrounded a perfect sun.

I averted my eyes from its overpowering glare.

I glanced down at the girl.

The wind tossed her hair. My skin was sensate again.

She was watching the planet and the sun perform their duet.

Scorching rays beat down on my face and I stood up, but the girl sat protected in the shade.

I couldn't see her face.

With a flash, the white sun burst into reddish flames, a conflagration of orange. The landscape twisted and quivered under the blaze.

A flock of birds flew into the distortion.

I could no longer tell whether it was dawn or dusk.

I woke up in my room. The morning sun shone in through the thin curtains.

I washed my face, changed into my school uniform, skipped breakfast, and rode my Cub to school. No one was there yet. I went to the archery grounds and opened the shutters to the shooting hall and target area. I grabbed my carbon Higo Sozan bow and duralumin arrows. When I entered the hall from the left and readied my bow, the morning sunlight poured onto my feet. The red tinge that spread over Tanegashima was much fainter than the light I had seen in my dream.

I didn't have *kyudo* practice the morning of my dream but had come anyway.

I was probably trying to avoid confusing its images with the sounds, smells, and sensations of my everyday life.

I don't even know when I first had that dream. Yet one day, I noticed that it was *recurring.*

A dream where I was with an unknown girl, on a planet that wasn't Earth. I could see the landscape so clearly that I could draw it, but my impression of the girl was disturbingly vague. I couldn't tell who she was. It was as if only her presence was there.

I think the landscape in my dream was roughly based on Tanegashima. You found broad hills like that almost anywhere on the island.

But I had never seen binary planets or distorting suns with my own eyes.

What in this world made me have that dream?

In that landscape, I felt fulfilled.

It had everything I sought. All that I wished for but couldn't express was forcefully etched into that world.

If I could go there…

I would throw everything else away.

I wouldn't need my parents, my friends, a home to return to, or a future—not a single thing.

I loved that place.

I loved whatever it was that imbued that place.

Every time I opened my eyes and got dragged back to reality, I was beset by a sense that I was incomplete.

I would take big gulps of water straight from the faucet until I was in pain.

Then I'd realize that the back of my throat wasn't itchy because I was thirsty.

It was because an important piece of me was missing.

The dream was the missing piece that fit exactly in place. It was trying to tell me something. Some unknown part of me was issuing a threat. I had better search for it, that self warned; I would only ever wake to empty mornings until I found it and made it mine.

After I had shot arrows until my arms were too shaky to grip the bow, I started typing out a message on my cell phone. I'd developed the habit of logging my dreams so I wouldn't forget them.

The hazy nebula staining the heavens, the unnaturally beautiful light green of the low sky, and the warmth of a girl by my side, never more than an impression.

I recorded every last bit of the scenery, from beginning to end. Then without meaning to, but quite naturally, I concluded with the question, "Who are you?"

That was when I realized I was transcribing the dream so that I could share it with someone.

I wanted to tell someone something.

That strong desire lay dormant inside me.

Telling someone something.

Only that someone would understand.

It was all so vague.

Who did I want to talk to? And what did I want to say? I couldn't find the answers. Like some dream I had forgotten upon waking, they lay beyond my consciousness.

Done composing, I fiddled with my cell, and then like always deleted the message.

I felt nostalgic when I thought about Akari Shinohara, but that was about it. I had a daily routine, various matters to attend to. I had no choice but to think of her as belonging to my past, which really wasn't that hard for me to do.

I was struggling to get through each and every day. I had no time to reflect on the past.

Yet I sometimes felt a presence, saw a figure in the corner of my eye, and would stop dead in my tracks.

It felt as if someone's shadow, or spirit, was watching me from not far away.

I would squint my eyes, but no one was ever there. Kanae shot me a puzzled look every time I abruptly turned my head and glared into empty space.

"Shadow" isn't the right word; it was no more there than a breath of air.

I only knew that the breath felt kind to me.

Generally, I was regarded as a decent, sociable guy who didn't make any waves.

A thin, invisible wall always separated me from my surroundings, but I built perfectly amicable relationships across it.

A shadow was being cast into that gap, the narrow margin of error that only Kanae seemed to register. I didn't know whose it was. I wasn't even sure what it was trying to tell me.

"Who are you?" I occasionally asked the shadow lurking in the gap at the edge of my world, when no one was around.

Pretty gloomy of me, if I do say so myself.

<h1 style="text-align:center">8</h1>

Although there were a few minor complications, getting a Cub was definitely the right decision.

With it, I could go anywhere on the island. A huge plus was that I could get to Nishinoomote, on the northern tip, anytime I liked. The most developed city on Tanegashima, it was the only place I could buy anything other than necessities. You even had to go through its port if you wanted to leave for Kagoshima City.

Now that I had a motorcycle, there was suddenly so much more I could do.

My mindset changed subtly as a result.

A greater reach meant more for the taking. It was as if my arm had grown longer.

I felt bigger. I'd been granted greater freedom to take what I liked.

One time, I spent an entire Sunday circling the island. I had done that on my bike a few years back, but this time was totally different.

On my bike, I had desperately followed the route suggested in my guidebook. With my Cub, though, I could go down any road. I went where I pleased, easily.

It made life exciting.

Maybe I'll get a car next.

It was a natural thought.

The next step. How far would my domain extend? Just the idea made my heart race.

But then I'd remember: I couldn't leave the island by motorcycle or car…

And my daydreams would always stop there.

When I was feeling blue, I would ride my Cub along the seaside cliff road, from the Hirota Ruins to the Space Center. The wind always felt nice against my body. The scent of the ocean was always refreshing.

With the extreme ups, downs, and curves, cars rarely ever took the road. In Kanto, street racers would have definitely made it their home track.

While I wished my Cub were more powerful uphill, when I looked to the sea on my left and lent my body to the cresting road, I felt like I had left behind all my troubles.

If I got tired, I would lean against the flimsy fence along the cliffs and smoke.

If I stared out into space for an hour, breathing as slowly as I could, my heart started to link to another channel.

There were a few places on the island where I could be alone.

Once, heading to such a spot, I ran into Kanae.

When was that again? She had already switched from bodyboarding to surfing, so it must have been after the summer of my second year in high school. She'd gone for the real deal saying she wanted to stand on those waves.

Since the island's population density was so low, there were hardly any people where I hung around. I seldom ran into my classmates outside of school.

Riding down a narrow road south from the center of Minamitane, I came across a familiar-looking Cub parked on the side of the road. It was Kanae's.

Each Cub wore dirt in a slightly different way, so it was surprisingly easy to tell whose Cub was whose.

I couldn't see her anywhere, so I decided to take a look around.

I had been riding aimlessly and not noticed that I was near an elementary school. I couldn't see or hear any children, though. The two-story building was made of reinforced steel but in terrible condition.

Did it close down?

I went through the steel gates and trespassed onto the grounds.

I found Kanae right away. She was sitting, with her legs out, on a bench in a corner and staring into space.

"Tohno…" she muttered distractedly. It was rare to see such a subdued reaction from her.

"Weird spot you chose," I remarked, ambling up to her.

"Yeah. I come here every once in a while. Like when I'm feeling worn out."

Sounds like something I would do, I thought.

I took what she said at face value and figured she must have been beat. I honestly felt sorry for her. A lively girl like her looking weary seemed so wrong.

"This," she announced abruptly, "is where I went to elementary."

"Huh, you don't say."

"But now it's completely closed."

"It sure does seem that way."

This time I got a good look at the building. The dark-red paint on the stark concrete walls was almost entirely faded and peeling.

"The schools you know don't have bare concrete walls like this, do they?"

"Can't say they do."

"It's because of the typhoons. It's too dangerous to put down mortar or tiles. We just paint directly onto the concrete. Seeing my school all bleak and abandoned like this…makes me feel really lonely."

Elementary schools were being shut down and consolidated due to the area's declining population, but it hadn't affected a junior high transfer like me.

A heartfelt recollection on the part of a morose Kanae, however, persuaded me that it was a serious issue.

"You're lonely?" I asked, all too directly.

"Yeah," Kanae admitted without ado. "I mean, I was here for six years, from when I was seven years old. I have a lot of memories of this school. It's sad to lose a place filled with so many."

"I see." I nodded, but the words that flowed out of my mouth next surprised me. "I'm kinda jealous."

"Why?"

"Because I don't know what that feels like. I've pretty much hopped from school to school my whole life. I don't think there's a single place I feel sentimental about."

"You don't wanna go back to Tokyo?"

"Tokyo? Why?"

"You just seem like you want to go back. That's what people are saying, anyway."

"I don't have any special attachment to the place, though."

"But aren't you planning to go to college in Tokyo?"

"Yeah, but not for any specific reason. Tokyo's pretty much the main hub of Japan. When in doubt, stay in the center."

"Wow, you're so…decisive…"

"I guess if that's what you wanna call it."

Kanae pinched and twisted her fingers for a minute. I suppose she needed something to be moving while she was thinking—to remind herself that time was passing.

"Hey, how can I be decisive like you?"

"What do you mean?"

"I can't decide anything."

"You're deciding plenty. Like deciding to surf and stuff."

"Actually, my older sister surfed, so it's just another hand-me-down. What do I wanna do? Where should I go? I have no idea…"

"You're saying you can't decide where to go to college?"

"Well, that too, but…"

"You mean more in a general sense?"

"Yeah, I think so. Which is why I'm panicking."

"Panicking?"

"It's scary…"

"What's scary?"

"Not being able to make decisions because I don't know what I want. And also watching other people make decisions."

"Ah…"

I got what she was saying. Finally.

And I could relate to her, and sympathize with her.

Not knowing what you want to do or become. Not being able to decide. Lacking the basis for it.

What is most valuable to you? What can't you let go of? What would you risk it all to achieve?

She was stuck because she couldn't answer those questions.

She didn't know why she couldn't decide, when her classmates made it look so easy.

It might sound a bit cheesy, but Kanae had *no dreams to dream.*

Hence her panic.

I knew exactly how scary that could be.

Maybe I was making hasty decisions to avoid facing that fear.

Her classmates were probably just the same.

I realized something.

Come to think of it, it's normal for people not to know what they want.

Maybe I just didn't want to accept that in myself.

Influenced by the mood, the media, and such.

Our environment—society, in other words—says to *hold on to your dreams.* Television, magazines, and fashion innocuously push the *wonders* of making your dreams come true.

Everyone is convinced that having a purpose is priceless.

Kanae was suffering from that belief.

"It's the same thing with surfing," she said. "I only reached for it because it was close by. I didn't care what, I just thought I might change if I tried something new. So I had my older sister teach me how to surf."

"I see."

"But I guess it's no use. I can't even stand on the board yet. Whatever it is, you need to have your life together to do it well. You know, it's not like I need to surf or anything. Maybe I should just give up—"

"You absolutely mustn't," I interrupted.

"What?" Sitting up straight, Kanae looked at me as if she had just woken up.

"You might know not where you're going, but that doesn't mean you won't make it somewhere. Just because you can't feel yourself moving forward doesn't mean that you aren't."

"What do you mean?" Now she seemed confused.

"As long as you persevere, you'll arrive somewhere eventually. No matter where that might be, I think having the ability to say you did your best to get there is enough of an accomplishment. Even if you don't end up where you thought you would, moving forward is a victory in itself. By the way, Homan Shrine and the lake are right around the corner, aren't they? You know, the red-rice shrine."

"Huh? Oh, yeah. What about it?"

A Tanegashima tourist spot, Homan was a shrine to the goddess of rice harvests. Near it was a freshwater lake.

"If you dive deep enough, you can swim all the way to a grotto on Madate Beach."

"What? No way! The lake and the grotto are connected?"

"No, that's just legend. The only thing connecting them, actually, is our imagination."

"Wow, you surprised me there. How did you hear about that legend?"

"What I'm trying to say is that sometimes things can connect in unexpected ways. When you look back on things, you marvel at how far you've traveled, and maybe where you ended up is the right answer after all. So just keep moving forward and don't stop. If you do, you won't go anywhere."

"I've never seen you talk so much before," Kanae said, off-topic, after looking stunned for a moment.

"I'm not all that quiet, okay? I talk when there's something to talk about."

She didn't specifically agree or disagree with my outlook. I guess if cheering her up were that easy, her troubles wouldn't have been serious in the first place.

"I've never heard of that legend before. How am I only hearing about this from you now when I've lived here my whole life?"

Because this is your hometown. Locals can't see their backyard from a tourist's point of view.

Of course, I didn't voice that thought.

I was beginning to sympathize deeply with Kanae's fears and anxieties.

Too many people are careless when it comes to their goals, hopes, and dreams.

Too many people ask, "What do you want to be?"

I don't want to answer those fools.

I don't want to have to put my dreams into words.

It's strange how people don't know what they lose when they put an idea into words.

Why do they try to make me define something that only exists in vague terms?

Why do they want to destroy something so formless, so important by defining it?

They have no idea what true beauty is.

Things of true value have no definite form.

Those hostile ideas unfurled in my head.

My own speech to Kanae made me anxious.

Had I accidentally said something fatal to myself?

Would I eventually get somewhere if I persevered?

What couldn't I let go of?

I hoped swimming through a dark water tunnel really got me someplace else.

Would I actually be okay with not ending up where I wanted?

Did I truly believe that?

What did I want to choose?

Nothing.

I had always known that there was nothing worth choosing.

"I really admire my big sister…" Kanae said. "If I'm not careful, I might become just like her without even noticing it."

"Is that bad?"

"Yeah. I think it is. I don't know, it just bothers me. I don't like when people compare us."

"I'm an only child, so I don't know how that feels."

"I do love my big sis, I just can't stand the pressure. After she graduated high school, she went straight to Fukuoka University, got her teaching license, became a teacher right away, and then came back home. That's what I have to live up to. I even have to see her at school."

Miho Sumida, you mean.

Ms. Sumida, a new teacher who arrived the same year that we entered our high school.

"Well, we're keeping it a secret for now. Bet you never would've guessed we're sisters."

Contrary to Kanae's assumption, I already knew. I had spoken privately with Ms. Sumida on a couple of occasions.

7

It was in the evening, not long after I had started my first year of high school. I was riding my Cub home when it unexpectedly stalled in the middle of the deserted country road.

I repeatedly kicked the starter, but the engine showed no sign of life. It wouldn't even rev.

I was still quite far from home. As the darkness thickened around me, I tried to figure out my next move when a passing car, an old hatchback, pulled over on the side of the road. A young woman stepped out from the driver's side.

"What's up?" she asked.

"My Cub isn't working."

"Hmm, I see it's new," she said, examining my Cub. "You sure it's not out of gas?"

She spoke in a no-frills, straightforward manner. "Everyone over-estimates the Cub's mileage. Most first-timers don't know when to re-fuel. I see it all the time. I'll take you to the gas station and back so you can buy yourself some gasoline."

"Thank you so much. Are you sure it isn't too much trouble..." Just then, I realized who I was speaking to. "Ms. Sumida?"

"Ahh, I *thought* you were one of our students. I'm glad I was passing through. You carrying cash?"

"Yeah, a little bit."

Barely making sure that I had shut my door, Ms. Sumida stepped on the accelerator. The headlight beams chased off the darkness as we continued down the farm road. LINDBERG's "I BELIEVE IN LOVE" was playing in the car.

"This song takes me back," I said.

"Huh? Er, yeah, it was really popular when I was young. But you?" Ms. Sumida asked suspiciously.

"It's nostalgic for me."

"I used to do it too, but don't all high schoolers say that things are 'nostalgic' without really meaning it?"

"That's probably true. I lived in an apartment where this song

128

sometimes played on the USEN radio. This song and the view I had from the veranda are sort of linked together in my memory."

"Where did you live before?"

"Tokyo…and various other places."

"Oh jeez, I can't even tell dialects apart anymore," Ms. Sumida said, scratching the steering wheel. "Just a little while ago, I could tell the difference between a newcomer and a local in one try. Everyone's dialect is getting softer."

We arrived at the gas station. After I borrowed a jerry can and filled it, Ms. Sumida drove me back to the spot where she had found me.

"It's not like there are any temptations along the way, so I guess just take care scooting home," she said through the open car window. Then, without any sort of gesture, she faced forward and promptly took off.

Ms. Sumida wasn't one to waste time. In fact, she hadn't even checked if my tank was really empty.

I opened and refilled the tank and tried turning on the engine.

It started on the first shot.

I ran into Ms. Sumida again a few months later on a Sunday. I was eating lunch at a hamburger joint before going to Nishinoomote for some shopping, when someone barged into the wooden-floored establishment, called out my name, and took a seat across from me. It was her.

"Are you on island patrol today?" I dreaded having to deal with her of all people but spoke as politely as I could.

"Hell no. I don't get paid enough to search for mischievous kids on my day off," she grumbled before ordering a coffee. "Well… I was just passing by and happened to spot you, so I figured this was the perfect opportunity to get a good look at your face."

"My…face?"

"Yes."

"Why?"

"Why do you think?"

After thinking for about five seconds, an answer came to me. "Are you related to Kanae?"

"That was fast. You're a quick guesser."

"Wait, so you two are actually related?" I was pretty shocked.

"We're not just relatives, we're sisters. A lot of Sumidas around these parts—I thought it might be harder to guess."

She was right. Until that moment, I had never connected Kanae with Ms. Sumida. Common sense had also ruled out the idea; a teacher wouldn't be working at a school that a family member would attend.

"That's pretty rare for a public school," I remarked.

"I don't have a choice. There aren't a lot of high schools on the island. On the mainland, I'd be transferred in a heartbeat. For now we're just hiding that we're sisters, but we're not going to deny it if someone points it out."

I then carefully put out feelers on me and Kanae.

"I hope there hasn't been any sort of misunderstanding about…"

"None. Don't worry," Ms. Sumida said with a wry smile. "Long story short, this one time when Kanae came home late, I noticed a certain boy had made sure she'd be safe. When I secretly peeked at his face, he looked very familiar."

She openly admitted to using her teacher privileges to check the roster and find out my name.

"Then I remembered that during my visits back home when I was in college, Kanae used to talk about this kid who had moved here from Tokyo. She's so easy to figure out, it's almost impressive."

It seemed that there was a misunderstanding, after all. I felt uncomfortable deep down but kept quiet.

My name must have come up in various other households when I first transferred in. Around these parts people lived in a frighteningly small world. A fresh chill ran down my spine.

"Were you convinced I was that boy when you saw my face?"

"What I thought is neither here nor there. I guess it did satisfy my curiosity."

"Then would you mind if I asked you something?"

"Not at all, what's up?"

"How do you become a teacher?"

"You need to go to college and get your teaching degree. If you've already picked teaching as your vocation, you enroll in the education program at your university. Recently, it's tough to find a teaching job without a master's degree. It also has a lot to do with which college you graduate from. You should ask your guidance counselor about it for more detailed information. So, you want to be a teacher?"

"I don't think so."

"Then why'd you ask?"

"Just for reference, I guess."

Ms. Sumida tilted back her head a little, perhaps to take a good, long look at me. "Isn't there something else you want to ask?"

I ended up feeling intimidated by Ms. Sumida throughout high school, but this was the exact moment that did it.

She was the toughest cookie I had ever met. I couldn't handle much more of her seeing through me.

"You went to Fukuoka University, right? Why did you come back to the island after graduating?" That was what I really wanted to ask. "Did you plan to work on Tanegashima from the beginning?"

"Actually, I didn't. It just kind of happened that way. I could have stayed in Kyushu forever."

"Why didn't you take that opportunity?"

After pausing to think, Ms. Sumida quietly continued, "Because my relationship fell apart. If it hadn't, I don't think I would have come back."

My mouth hung half-open. I was at a loss for words.

I was stunned that she could fairly offhandedly share that personal detail with a young student like me. Moreover, I felt flustered because she seemed to be trying to warn me in some way.

"I guess you could say that we marched to two different beats," Ms. Sumida said, not sounding particularly solemn. Her tone hadn't changed throughout our conversation. "If a relationship is only about the now and can't proceed, it's not going to work. It's over when you can tell that it's a lost cause. At the time, I hadn't taken charge of my life and didn't know what to do with our relationship."

Her story was too real for a boy in a provincial high school to fully understand.

"But you don't know what that feels like, do you?" she asked, sensing my confusion.

"It's like two passing trains..." I blurted out. I had no idea why I came up with that metaphor.

"Passing trains?"

"In other words, two trains that are going opposite ways on parallel tracks. They're perfectly aligned for a moment, but the moment only exists at that one time, in that one place, and can't be taken anywhere..."

Ms. Sumida looked at me with a glint of surprise in her eyes.

"Er, I can't explain it well..." I said.

"Do you read a lot?"

"Much less than I used to."

"I think you're talking about something a little bit different, but still, it's weird how that metaphor just came out of your mouth. It's kind of creepy. It's not like the kids in class think you're weird or anything."

"They do, though."

"No. I know that for a fact."

"May I finish asking my question?"

"Sure. Go ahead."

"Out of all the places in Japan, did you specifically choose to work on Tanegashima because you were used to the lifestyle here? Or did you feel like there was something on this island that you couldn't find anywhere else?"

I think I expected her to say the latter.

"I guess I did it to convince myself that all places are the same," Ms. Sumida answered. "Thinking there's something else out there is basically just a fantasy. I suppose I'm trying to confirm that. I couldn't wait to get off this humdrum island when I was your age, though."

She also happily added that working on the island meant that she could surf. Then, she muttered that it hadn't been anything to tell a high school kid whose whole future was ahead of him.

"Do you surf? I can teach you."

"Actually, I've got my hands tied with my club right now."

"Uh huh. Archery?"

"You even researched that about me?"

"While you haven't asked a single thing about Kanae," Ms. Sumida pointed out casually.

She polished off her lukewarm coffee then said that she had one last reminder for me.

"I won't tell Kanae about today," I preempted.

"See, that's exactly what worries me about you."

Ms. Sumida scooped up both of our receipts with frightening ease and stood up. By the time I noticed what she was doing and shot out my hand, the two slips of paper were securely in her possession.

As I sat there baffled, she promptly paid our checks at the counter and breezed out of the restaurant.

I stayed there and sulked for a while, upset by Ms. Sumida's finishing blow. The problem—probably—was that my reach was far shorter than I'd hoped.

Besides my random encounters with Ms. Sumida, most of the days leading up to my final year of high school were pretty uneventful.

As usual, I shot arrows in the morning, headed to class, practiced again after school, went home, and studied as much as I thought was necessary. After continuing this cycle for more than two years, the summer of my eighteenth year arrived.

In the early mornings, before anyone else was at school, I would open the shutters to the *kyudo* grounds and shoot arrows at the targets.

It felt nice.

With no one watching, I could have easily fooled around and just shot off some arrows for fun (that kind of horseplay was popular at the time), but instead I moved exactly as the *kyudo* principles dictated, from the moment I entered the range until I exited.

Lending my body to the rigid shooting forms was oddly enjoyable.

I felt like I was eliminating my physical "noise" as an organism, discarding individual quirks that amounted to nothing, and optimizing my very being. It was like sharpening a pencil. I was honing my dull parts.

If I had to name any issues, well, I was horribly mediocre in the accuracy department. I "shot to hit," I was often told. Meaning that I was too focused on the outcome. It wasn't something I could fix on my own.

As I practiced alone in the early mornings, Kanae occasionally came to watch. In the course of chatting with her, I let down my guard and opened up to her about that and other things.

Every now and then, I had the dream.

The dream where the girl and I walk on a pale-green field.

Why was it never daytime, I wonder.

We would climb the hill.

The soft ground beneath my feet. The sound of our shoes parting the grass. It all felt real.

Insects flitted, the wind blew. The girl's hair danced in the breeze, and when it clung to her cheek, she brushed it away with a slightly annoyed gesture.

The landscape felt completely natural, but we weren't on Earth. That much I knew.

Undiscovered constellations. A plethora of stars. An ancient, looming sun.

The night sky always glowed with the light of countless purplish nebulae.

When I woke up, I realized I had never seen the girl's face. In the dream I could feel her very breath, yet I didn't know who she was. I also never considered the question while I was dreaming.

Getting out of bed, I would pick up my cell phone from my desk, go into email, and jot down the contents of the dream. Once I was done writing everything I could remember, I pressed delete.

"Erase this message?" the confirmation screen would ask me.

A feeling like a prayer flitted through me every time.

Although the message was deleted, it felt as if I had "sent it off to nowhere."

I was hoping it would travel through a supernatural circuit and arrive someplace…

The *kyudo* club adjourned for the day, but I stayed behind to shoot some arrows by myself. I was packing my things in the parking lot when Kanae approached me.

"Are you done with practice, Tohno?"

"Yeah. What've you been up to?"

"I just came from the beach. My sister drove me back in her car."

"You're really giving it your all out there, aren't you," I marveled. I imagined Kanae had spent another afternoon tirelessly pushing through the waves.

"What? Oh, no, not really..." She flashed a shy smile.

"Wanna ride home together?"

"Sure."

We got on our Cubs, started our engines, and proceeded through the school gates at a leisurely pace. Just past the fire station at the end of the road, the residential street merged into the national highway. Turning at an intersection, we headed down the community road to Minamitane.

We nodded to each other at a stoplight and went down a side road to the Ai Shop, our usual hangout. It had become our routine to buy something there and chat whenever we rode home together.

Crouching in front of the drink section, Kanae pressed her finger against the chilly glass and carefully contemplated her choice of beverage.

I was somewhat conscious of her pale shoulders, petite frame, and thin neck. Her unguarded demeanor, right there below my eyes, aroused something inside me.

I didn't care which drink I bought and didn't want to waste time picking one out, so I just grabbed my usual coffee carton from Dairy (a local business).

"The same one again, Tohno?"

"You know, you always look so serious when you're picking one out."

"Well yeah, it's super important."

"I'll meet you outside," I said. I paid at the register and exited the store.

Kanae probably took that tiny detail to mean that she was always hesitant, while I wasn't at all.

My meaning, however, was that I lacked the drive to seek out what mattered to me, whereas she was the opposite.

Which was why I thought she was wonderful.

She was adorable, and I sometimes even felt envious.

Outside of the store, I sat on a bench labeled with an ice cream logo and pushed my straw into the coffee carton. Kanae came out of the shop and sat next to me.

She felt incredibly close.

The fabric of her school uniform grazed my arm.

Someone's warmth, right there next to me—it was a nostalgic feeling.

It almost melted my heart.

Just then, a thought floated across my mind: *What if Kanae is the girl from my dream?*

Wouldn't it be great…

If it were true?

Would I be stuck on that island forever? Would staying there ever mean anything to me?

I tried to talk to Kanae about it on many occasions.

I desperately needed to talk to someone who might understand what I was going through.

Yet every time I tried to bring it up, I was stunned by my inability to express myself.

No matter how hard I tried, the thin wall wouldn't let me.

My formless thoughts refracted around me.

The world rejected me past a certain point.

I still didn't want to deal with Miho Sumida, or "Ms. Sumida."

I stayed as far away from her as I could, but we ended up having one last encounter.

Since I was in my third and last year of high school, I had begun career counseling, which is where students meet with an advisor to talk about their future. The counselor just so happened to be out on "urgent business" that day, so I wound up with Ms. Sumida.

"I'm thinking of attending college in the Tokyo area," I expressed my vague hope.

"You mean you're not set on a specific school, but on being somewhere in Tokyo?" she said, twirling a pen. "It's not about getting into a particular college or program, but all about the direction?"

It was a fair question. "I can't picture where I'll end up unless I have a direction in mind."

She advised that given my fine academic standing, it wouldn't be too hard for me to get into a decent college in Tokyo. The counseling session soon finished up, and we started chatting.

"I just want to make a drastic move. Even Hokkaido would do, actually," I was confessing before I even noticed.

Ms. Sumida's openness during our last conversation must have rubbed off on me.

"I have this intense desire to move. Pretty much all the time," I said on a whim, but the moment I did, I knew it was the truth.

"Oh, I see... I wonder why that is."

"I'm not sure... But I feel like I've already seen everything here, and I want to find something new."

"I'm sorry, mind if I give my two cents?" Ms. Sumida said, putting down her pen. "You can't keep pushing forward like a wedge plow. That definitely won't last."

"Wedge plow?" *Wedge plow?*

"You know, the diesel-powered thing that pushes snow off railroad tracks. That yellow guy. I'm sure you've seen it on TV before."

"Oh, that thing..."

"When I meet students for career counseling, I think about who they remind me of out of the people I know. The first time I saw you, I thought of a senior of mine in college. She was a girl, though. She quit school and ran off to Canada without telling a soul."

"Canada?"

"She died in a mountain climbing accident the year before last."

"What?!"

My emotions usually don't show on my face, but I bet I winced that time.

"What are you trying to say?"

"I've only recently discovered that there are two types of kids who aren't a handful," Ms. Sumida continued, half-ignoring my question. "A girl like Kanae is easy to deal with, you can leave her alone and she'll be fine. But someone like you might fall off a cliff without anyone knowing. I'm very worried about you."

"I'm not going to fall off a cliff. I would never let that happen."

"No stargazing while you're walking." Ms. Sumida scowled and stared straight at me. "You could die."

5

I was dreaming.

The girl and I ascended the hill.

The starlit hill was a gentle green, the most endearing color to me. It wouldn't do if it were even a bit lighter or darker. The shading was just perfect.

The warmth that I could feel, but not touch.

We were the only ones in that beloved space.

Yes.

It was perfect.

As if the concept of perfection had taken form.

It was there in the dream.

It was there in my hands.

All of my hopes had finally materialized.

This was where I wanted to be. This was where I wanted to stay.

I wanted to hold the landscape.

The girl and the universe fully understood me.

And I fully understood them as well.

I was almost a grownup and knew that no such place existed.

I knew it, but couldn't accept it. I couldn't stop reaching into the darkness to find it.

One late-summer evening full of the cicadas' song, Kanae and I were riding home together on our motorcycles.

We were spending more and more time together.

The road home that had cooked us just a few days ago was blanketed in a cool breeze.

I never checked my side mirror. I didn't have to turn back to know she was there.

I only looked straight ahead.

I want to ride harder.

I want to ride faster.

That vector existed in me.

I could only keep going.

While Kanae stressed over drinks in the Ai Shop like always, I bought my usual Dairy coffee and stepped outside.

I leaned against the seat of my Cub, took out my phone, and continued to write down my dream, picking up where I had left off.

A message to nowhere.

Kanae came out. She faltered when she saw me.

She wanted to ask about the message. But she decided against it. That much I could figure out.

For a split second, I expected something. About her. From her. But...

I flat-out rejected that desire. I folded my flip phone with a snap.

We rode into the pitch-black night. I saw her off at her house.

When we parked our Cubs by the front gate, a small Shiba Inu leapt out from an old metal basin, and executing a drift along the way, jumped at Kanae.

"Hi, Cubb, I'm home! Oh, my Cubboo Wubboo!"

She bent down and gently scratched around the pup's collar. Its owner wore a lovely expression. So cute she couldn't stand it.

With deft footwork, Cubb played with Kanae's fingers from every possible angle.

"Cubb" was a nice name. Even if a dog has four legs while a Cub is a two-wheeler.

While I gazed at Kanae's back as she crouched and cheerfully petted Cubb, something clawed at my memory.

I started searching my dream for the memory, but that wasn't it. The sense of déjà vu was connected to a more realistic picture.

A haze obscured that memory-like thing, and it immediately fell out of my grasp. All I was left with was a painfully sentimental, trembling feeling that made me want to cry.

Once, I wondered what would happen if I persuaded Kanae to sleep with me. I just might find something important through the act.

I know it was an inane and selfish idea. I rejected it partly because it seemed too complicated on many levels.

But that wasn't the biggest problem. I tossed out the idea mainly because she was dear to me.

While I didn't love her in a romantic sense, I did cherish her.

I didn't want to hurt her. I wanted to take care of her.

There was one more reason.

I was scared.

Scared that I wouldn't find anything important inside her.

Which is why I thought I shouldn't even try.

That decision absolutely crushed me. It was the final verdict: *There is nothing for you anywhere.*

Clearly, something about Kanae had deeply affected me. For many years, I couldn't decipher exactly what it was.

I only figured it out way after the fact. If I had to put how she made me feel into words, "nostalgic" is the closest I can get.

If I had been born and raised on that island and hadn't had the peculiar dream… I'm sure I would have fallen for a girl like Kanae.

I might have had my fulfilling childhood, full of uncertainty and pain and joy.

Envying that alternate version of myself in another world was like the heartache of a long-distance relationship.

4

In the dream, the hill continues.

Just when I think I've reached the top, I wake up.

Morning. I shot arrows at school. My accuracy was especially off that day.

I kept missing because there was something wrong with my posture.

"But I think you shoot beautifully."

Kanae had returned from the beach. I think she liked how something was always wrong with me.

The season where nothing but hot stuffy air wafted in through the windows was over, and I found myself smiling at the refreshing feeling of air moving against my skin.

I liked watching the thin curtains in the classroom dance in the wind. The high afternoon sunlight masked the area below the windows in shade. When the curtains swayed, it looked as if sunlight was being swept into the room.

We seniors barely had classes anymore and were left to study on our own for our college entrance exams. Not hearing people's voices was liberating. I was trying to sense my freedom in the breeze.

I skipped archery practice.

I think I felt the freest when I flipped up my kickstand in the parking lot.

I even felt free banking hard just for fun en route to the side gate.

I bought my usual carton of coffee from the usual shop. Then I chose to take a different route home than usual. I headed to the heart of the island, where it jutted farthest up out of the sea.

I shifted into low gear as I took a plain black asphalt road that was unmarked not just in the center, but on the sides.

It wasn't long before I reached the top of the winding path. There I turned onto a straight road that traced the ridge southward.

The entire road was on an elevated area, so I could see the sea stretching for miles east and west. The view was so breathtaking that a guidebook might list it as a scenic driving route.

I saw a gateball court and an observation deck along the way, but I just kept going.

After riding for a short while longer, I stopped.

I felt like taking in the scenery flowing past me.

On my right was a massive field. Tanegashima sweet potatoes—I could tell by the leaves' dark color and distinctive shape. I was crazy about Tanegashima potatoes.

The orderly lines of leaves were a bracing sight.

Riding down a narrow path between the fields, I reached a dirt embankment. The island had many similar artificial walls that had been erected to block the wind. The fields were tilled behind them.

I dismounted there and trotted up the embankment slope.

I inhaled.

Ah…

It reminded me so much of the place in my dream.

I moved forward.

If I kept going, what would I see?

My vista expanded when the ground receded.

A panorama suddenly opened up beneath me.

Under my eyes was a sweeping view of Tanegashima's southern plains.

On my left and right were dull grays, Minamitane and Nakatane. They both looked tiny. Nothing but varied hues of green filled the gap between the towns.

The yellow-green surface, which spread far out before me, was a sugarcane field.

The crop had a deep color seen from up close, but from my far-away viewpoint it looked light and gentle.

Lying low in the distance was a vast forest, dark green. Rather than constitute a simple plane, it drew intricate stripes that intertwined into a jet-black presence.

The light fields and dark woodlands created the complex color pattern of an abstract painting. The contrast between the flat fields and pop-up forests were reminiscent of a dynamic style done in oil.

There were pointy looking, light-green sections of bamboo grass in the windbreaks. They constituted a border that accented the blackness of the forest.

A nearby windbreak also swayed in the wind.

Directing my gaze into the distance, where the plains broke off, I saw a flimsy liquid surface. Namely the sea.

Above the sea was the sky, of course.

An enormous sky. There aren't many places in Japan with a sky as broad as that.

Lattice towers with uniform orientations stood in a neat line.

Then, on the far left, I saw something that caught me off guard.

A pure-white windmill with three blades.

It was the only part of the scenery that was moving in a definite manner.

The tower, which gradually thinned out towards the top, protruded from the space between the forests. Its three blades, positioned at four, eight, and twelve o' clock, looked sharp enough to slice your hands off.

The white blades slowly turned.

They seemed to have caught a nice breeze.

Although the wind turned the blades, when I stared at them long enough, it felt as if they were motor-operated and generating the air-flow instead.

I was seeing the windmill in a new light. A sort of monument and symbol of a public fitness center—The Solar Village—I had actually looked up at it from its base many times before.

Viewed from far away, however, it looked strangely forlorn, and yet powerful, swallowing my gaze.

I watched the windmill turn for a few moments before sitting down on the grass embankment. The weeds undulated in the wind. The breeze felt so nice that I felt like lying down.

I began leaning back when I remembered that my cell was in my back pocket.

I took it out and started a new message out of habit.

I hadn't written yet about the dream from the night before. I forgot about lying down and began writing.

How many times did I log those meaningless dreams?

Every time I wrote them down, I got frustrated and upset with myself for failing to reproduce even a glimpse of what I had seen.

Why did I record my dreams, only to delete them? Beats me too.

As I kept typing, the sky darkened around me. The backlight on my cell phone grew gradually brighter.

I heard a motorcycle down by the road but figured it was just a farmer who had come to tend the fields.

Soon after, I heard footsteps.

"Tohno," Kanae called out to me. I was surprised to hear her voice.

"Hey, Sumida. What's up? How'd you find me out here?"

"I saw your motorcycle and thought I'd stop by. Mind if I joined you?"

"Not at all. I didn't see you in the parking lot today. I'm glad you came by."

"Me too."

She jogged over and sat on the ground to my left. She removed her shoulder bag and put it down.

In telling her I was happy to see her, I was being quite genuine. This situation gave me déjà vu, which I guess made it easy to be honest about how I felt. I put away my phone and, keeping Kanae in the corner of my eye, gazed at the white windmill, which had started to light up in the meantime.

"So, Tohno, what have you been doing up here?"

"I was watching the windmill. You get a really nice view of it from here."

"What's it for?"

"Huh? You don't know?"

"Nope."

"It generates power, of course."

"Power? You mean it makes electricity?"

"Right."

"But how could it when it moves so slowly? Shouldn't it be going a lot faster?"

"Well, there are gears inside it that speed it up. Just like a bicycle. It takes a whole lot of wind pressure to move heavy blades like those. Wind power isn't about the speed of the wind, but its weight."

"Oh, wow…"

"The blades make turning round and round look easy, but I think they might actually be under a ton of pressure."

"How much electricity do you think it makes?"

"I looked it up the other day, but I forget the exact figure. Though I once heard they can make enough electricity to power an entire zoo."

"Really? Does that mean the park over there doesn't have to pay utilities?"

"Probably not. Though their bill might not actually be zero."

"Impressive… I wonder why wind power isn't more popular."

"That's because you can never fully pay off the maintenance and construction fees. Even if it spins until the end of its service life, I don't think it'll ever make enough energy to cover the costs…"

"Oh, so it's a complete waste, then."

"It's not a waste," I said quietly.

"Why not?"

I went silent. I couldn't come up with a good reason.

"Because it's beautiful," I replied.

It tirelessly catches the wind, stands in place, and spins, and that's beautiful.

I think that was the best possible answer I could have given to her question.

Kanae gestured, however, that she didn't quite get it.

"Hey, you're about to take entrance exams, right, Tohno?"

Mighty clouds floated in the vast blue darkening sky.

"Yeah. For colleges in Tokyo."

"Right, okay… That's what I thought."

"Why?" I asked, simply curious.

"You just seem like you wanna go far away."

I tried to hide that I was a little flustered by her comment. "How about you, Sumida?"

"Hmm…" she said, "I don't even know what I'm doing tomorrow."

"I'm pretty sure everyone feels that way."

A small bolt of lightning flashed in a faraway cloud.

"What?! Even you?"

"Of course."

She stared at my profile. I couldn't make out her expression since it had gotten fairly dark by then. But I could tell that her face was still saying "What?!" in disbelief.

"You don't seem worried about anything."

"No way. Worries are all I have."

The wind was blowing. The blades were spinning.

"I'm just doing what I can. Staying afloat," I said, looking toward the windmill. I meant that, one hundred percent.

"Oh, okay…"

Kanae sounded somewhat relieved. She took out a white piece of paper from the bag she had put on the ground. She seemed to be in high spirits. It seemed to be a printout of something. She started making origami.

"A paper airplane?"

"Mm-hm."

Kanae was the picture of contentment as she made precise folds on her knees. Her nails were very pretty. I watched her fingers move accurately as they transformed the piece of paper into a three-dimensional triangle.

After she extended and leveled the wings, she raised the paper airplane over her head and, probably feeling good about herself, tossed it into the wind.

It flew a lot straighter and farther than I expected.

Liberating.

Gliding over the gentle slope of the hill, it whirled up to a certain height before swooping down at the tiny townscape.

Then it soared up again, towards the shimmering stars.

Well, no… My hopes probably just made it look like it had flown into the stars.

I probably felt one with the airplane and was trying to propel my consciousness far, far away.

3

On the way back, a large trailer from the Space Center slowly traversed the pitch-black road.

I had decided to leave the embankment and escort Kanae home as usual because it felt like it was going to rain.

Right before the small farm road merged into two traffic lanes on the national highway, I thought I saw flashing red lights in the distance.

Naturally, I assumed it was an ambulance.

A guard with a safety jacket and red lamp took his position in the middle of the road before we could cross over. We slowed down and came to a halt at the stop line just before the intersection.

He lowered his sign and instructed us to wait. Kanae and I parked next to each other at the stop line and did as we were told.

Come to think of it, there was this deep, unfamiliar humming sound from the start. However, I didn't make much of it.

A massive object came into view from the right.

When I finally saw what it was, the hairs stood up on the back of my neck.

The trailer was freakishly huge. It was an incredibly unreal, mind-numbing sight.

There was no way something that massive was allowed on the road. It didn't even fit between the traffic lines. It took up the entire road and still needed more space.

It wasn't normal even in terms of height. It was sure to crash into stoplights. It would sever phone lines. Was it going to push through without even caring?

It wasn't until I saw the NASDA logo on the side that I realized what it was. After the logo went by, there was a coupling followed by a large ivory-colored box.

Containers linked into a rectangle.

So enormous that it made the trailer truck look small.

It moved before my eyes, just twenty feet away. A metallic wall had suddenly obstructed my view.

Right, of course.

A trailer transporting the H-IIA rocket, built by Mitsubishi Heavy Industries.

I had seen a picture of the rocket at the Space Center.

But I hadn't known it was this big.

I remembered a few things about the rocket. The space consortium's H-IIA was completed at a dock in Aichi Prefecture, then transported by boat to Shimama Port, on the south side of Tanegashima. The port was connected to the Space Center by a single prefectural road.

To ensure the safe passage of rocket-carrying trailers, no phone lines crossed the prefectural road. The traffic lights shut down and retracted to the side whenever a trailer was coming through.

In other words, special traffic regulations had to be instituted to accommodate these trailers. Southern Tanegashima had taken every possible measure to allow for the transport of rockets.

The flashing yellow warning lights on the trailer's roof lent a solemn air to the surrounding darkness.

A low-frequency bass dominated the area. The couplings occasionally let out metallic creaking sounds as if to chime in with the song.

A powerful light illuminated the entire trailer and its environs. Several guardsmen carefully monitored the road conditions.

The small flashes of lightning falling from the cumulonimbus clouds over the distant sea had no hold on me whatsoever; it was nothing compared to the immense mass moving before me.

The trailer sluggishly, painfully sluggishly, continued its journey.

The guards could have easily caught up to and passed it with a light jog, but they probably didn't want the tiniest vibration to mess with their precious rocket. They must have been worried about the natural frequency, or whatever. Even the guards escorting Hannibal Lecter weren't so vigilant.

The rocket mustn't deteriorate one bit before its safe launch into space—that firm will had turned into an enormous mass moving solemnly before me.

"…What?"

I looked back at Kanae.

"Five kilometers per hour," her profile repeated. She, too, was gazing at the trailer.

A chill crept near my feet, which the lights illuminated too.

"They said it travels to the Minamitane launch site at a speed of five kilometers per hour."

"Ah…"

I nodded casually—or pretended to have.

It wasn't easy. I had been shot straight through the heart, and I knew it.

The damage…

Slowly spread through my entire body.

I didn't understand why it hurt so much to hear those words.

Amidst the chaos, a number of feelings came back to me. I felt like I had shared something important with someone long ago.

We had tried to protect each other and team up against the world that way.

I nearly burst into tears.

I held them back.

Something in me would break if I cried. I didn't want to cry at all.

"There's going to be a launch this year. The first one in a while," Kanae said.

The trailer and container had passed us, and the lights, which had illuminated the area like a stage, were also receding. Even after the "Road Closed" sign was removed, Kanae and I stood there for a while in complete silence.

The line of light slowly faded into the darkness.

"Yeah, they say it's going to the outer reaches of the solar system…" I answered calmly even as a storm raged in me.

A few raindrops trickled down the glass shield of my motorcycle helmet.

"…It'll take years."

My eyes stayed glued to the back of the container as it silently made its exit.

The guards swung their red lights as they accompanied it on foot.

An emergency vehicle followed the trailer, lighting it up from behind.

The fortress of light slowly receded into the darkness.

That night, I had the dream again.

When I reached the top of the hill, the ocean expanded beneath me.

There was a curve in the sandy white beach.

I was there with the girl.

We stood there and listened to the waves, and watched them lap our feet. We glanced down at the foam timidly running away.

The ocean shone a metallic blue in the shadowy night.

That blue reflected the darkness of the sky.

The stars that looked like frosted glass in the zenith.

The dully twinkling lenticular nebula.

The surface reflected them.

A field of stars.

Normally, it was unthinkable on a rippling surface, but here I could fully accept it to be true.

Ahh, I had a realization.

This is where the rocket should land. The probe it carried would launch deep into space.

This is the landscape he needs to encounter.

The silver-blue ocean.
The rounded horizon emanated light.
Clouds spread along the horizon.
The low sky was green.
The high sky was a deep blue.
Ring-shaped clouds.
Then, a presence that took an eternity to arrive.
A truly lonely journey that defied the imagination.
Forging through genuine darkness—
Rarely meeting even a single hydrogen atom—
Simply believing in the esoteric abyss—
Wholeheartedly wishing to draw closer to the secrets of the universe.

I was aware. Aware that my consciousness being here was a miracle.
Aware of the miracle of her being next to me.
I was aware.
Aware of the passage of time.
Of the rustling of her soft cardigan.
Of her long, flowing skirt.
Of her hair.
Below the light green sky, under the umbrella of the lenticular nebula.
I looked at her profile.
The wind blew.
She seemed to be enjoying the breeze.
Who are you?

Wholeheartedly wishing to draw closer to the secrets of the universe.
How far will I go?
How far can I go?

2

Autumn came.

I lost a little weight. I walked only looking straight ahead.

I think I sensed something that day. Something big was going to happen. Should I welcome it or not? I didn't know. But I felt it coming. Then my premonition came true.

It wasn't so much intuition as a preconscious observation. At a seemingly imperceptible level, that day felt unlike any other. A black box mechanism in me was sending me warning signals.

Anyway, I was on edge that day. Maybe it was the stress of upcoming college exams; maybe a boring teacher had made a boring remark. On that kind of day, even the "Follow Your Path" slogan on the wall rubbed me the wrong way.

Which is why I felt so relieved when I met Kanae in the parking lot that evening. I had been more wound-up than I thought, my nerves as taut as a bow pulled back to its limit.

Kanae might have been lying in wait for me. When I arrived at the lot, I spotted her gazing in my direction from behind the school building. "Sumida?" I called out to her.

Surprised, she hurriedly showed herself.

"Heading home now?" I asked.

"Yeah."

"Nice." I cracked a smile. "Let's ride home together."

With a golden light slanting in, the convenience store had a nostalgic air that evening.

A sentimental song that I could have sworn I had heard somewhere was playing.

Kanae crouched in the drink corner as usual, but there was something different about her today. She was trying to sense something with her skin. She peered at my reflection in the glass door.

I opened the door and grabbed a carton of Dairy's Coffee.

Kanae always took a while to choose a drink, but today she found one almost immediately.

"Oh, already picked your drink today?"

"Yeah."

At that point, I think I already knew what was going to happen next.

She and I paid at the register and exited the store.

The evening light didn't touch the old bench, which was in the building's shadow, and it was dim there.

As she trailed behind me, Kanae's breathing sounded peculiar.

I felt some sort of physical resistance and stopped in place.

When I realized that she was grabbing my sleeve, the core of my body immediately grew chilly.

Insects squirmed inside me.

I was "rejecting" her.

I knew what she was going to say next.

I could anticipate the exact phrases and even how she would say them. Just imagining it made my stomach churn.

Don't.

You definitely shouldn't.

If I hear you say it, my interest in you will die for sure.

Which is why...

"Yeah?"

I turned around.

Quietly, but intimidatingly.

"Uh..."

Kanae placed her left hand on her chest and took a hesitant step backwards.

"What's wrong?" I asked in a very soft, impossibly calm voice.

She took a decisive step backwards.

Then she lowered her head and fell silent.

Good.

Well done.

Please, never put it into words.

Things that take form only decay. I don't want anything concrete.

Don't corrode what's dear to me.

I'm searching for something that can't be put into words.

I could hear the chirping of insects.

Though the sun was setting, its rays still dyed the concrete an intense orange on that southern island.

Kanae mumbled something.

"What?" I asked, gently.

"Um, well…" She shook her lowered head. "Sorry…it's nothing."

Still, I believe some little thing in me died then.

We decided to head home, but Kanae's motorcycle wouldn't crank. With her helmet on, she repeatedly stepped on the kick-start, but the engine refused to ignite.

I idled my Cub and pulled it up next to her.

"Something wrong with it?"

"Yeah… Weird."

I bent down and peered at the engine. After running out of gas and getting stranded on the road a few years back, I had taught myself how to diagnose and service motorcycle issues.

This might sound contradictory, but inspecting her motorcycle, I realized that in fact I cared for Kanae Sumida quite a lot.

"No good?" she asked in a cute voice. She was asking about her Cub.

Somewhere deep down, I still wished that she was the girl from my dream.

"Hmm… I think the plug gave out. Is this a hand-me-down?"

"Yeah, it was my sister's."

"When you accelerated, would the engine sputter?"

"…I think so."

I was speaking to her in the gentlest voice possible, though with a different nuance than just now.

It was obvious from the very beginning that she wasn't the girl from my dream. Even so, I wanted to cherish the possibility that it might be her.

"You should leave it here today and have someone from home come pick it up tomorrow. We'll walk today," I said, my voice genuinely kind as I turned off my engine. I put down the kickstand and got off my Cub. I had never felt so kind in my entire life.

"Oh, I'll walk by myself! You can start heading home first." Panicking, Kanae waved her hands in front of her chest. Her cheeks were flushed, and she wore a troubled expression.

"It's only a short walk. And besides…"

I wanted the girl from my dream to be a real presence that existed on Earth.

I clung to the theory that Kanae might be her.

A part of me really did want to stay.

"…I kind of feel like walking today."

But it was no longer an option.

1

Surrounded by nothing but a breathtaking view of the fields, Kanae and I walked alone down the country road.

No cars or motorcycles passed by. We just walked on the asphalt in a straight line and headed to our town while the sun was setting.

The road's smooth curve was barely noticeable if you were walking, and the ocean came into view. When the angle changed, the sea hid from us just as unexpectedly.

A golden light shimmered on its surface in the distance. I passed by more short wooden phone poles than I could count.

Kanae walked behind me. I sensed that she was. The last of the summer cicadas hurled their metallic song into the air.

I gazed up at the sky as I walked.

Wispy clouds added some nuance to the upper half of the evening sky, which was slowly turning a deep shade of blue. The lower half was gently fading to bright white.

I walked straight ahead.

As if I were pulling Kanae down the borderline between day and night with an invisible rope, I walked straight ahead. A chilly sensation still lingered in my arm from when she had grabbed my sleeve.

I was sinking into my fantasies.

I wanted to go somewhere.

I think I truly loved that beautiful island.

I spent four and a half years in junior high and high school on Tanegashima. The island's heat, the island's air, the taste of the island's soil. I was quite aware that they had seeped into me.

Did I really have to go somewhere else, in spite of all that?

Did I have to move, seeking a vista that could never exist on Earth?

I already knew the answer.

It was the only way.

It was painfully clear to me.

I could only hope for a miracle and keep reaching further.

Like cast iron, my body had been molded that way whether I liked it or not. I was probably that type of machine. I was an object installed with that kind of mechanism.

There was a headwind.

Its whooshing grazed my earlobes.

All of a sudden, I couldn't hear the cicadas' chirps or Kanae's foot-steps anymore.

I couldn't?

I turned around to find Kanae standing still, quite a distance away—and my eyes opened wide.

She was crying.

Her head still bowed, she kept wiping away her tears with the base of her thumb.

"What's the matter?" I asked. There was no hidden meaning to my question.

"Sorry, it's nothing... I'm so sorry..."

I didn't know what she was apologizing for. She just kept apologizing, and I couldn't find the right words.

I approached her and went to touch her shoulder...

But lowered my hand.

Why was she crying?

A part of me warned that I mustn't realize why, but deep down I understood.

No doubt, her reason was the same as mine.

She was crying in my place.

There was something we couldn't stop seeking.

She and I pursued it—

Reached out for it—

And had our dreams dashed—

After which we could only hope for a miracle.

Though that was our bitter end, I probably wasn't going to cry. Which is why she was. Her reason, the same as mine. Crying my tears. Crying for two.

She would become my other half that I left behind on the island...

Kanae scrunched her face and tried to stop crying, which could only have the opposite effect. I knew this, and I'm sure she did too. Regardless, she tried. Sobbing, her tears flowing, shielding her face, she tried to stop. But her body wouldn't listen.

I kept watch over Kanae across that short distance, feeling as if I were watching myself cry.

The sky turned purple behind her.

I could feel the evening sink in.

That's when it happened.

0

The cicadas stopped singing.

My skin sensed the anomaly in the air.

The change was so distinct that I had to wonder if the world had blacked out.

Kanae lifted her head, glanced over my shoulder, and opened her eyes wide.

I turned around.

—There was light.

Far off on the horizon, another small sun came up from the Space Center.

The trembling ball of light floated up into the sky.

A dense, sticky-looking trail of smoke spread across the ground and curled itself around the foot of the mountains.

The thunderous roar finally began to reach our ears.

A ferocious sound struck the air, the adjacent air fluttered—

And my lungs shook.

The trail of smoke elongated and a blinding light climbed towards the zenith.

A white column seemed to be rising toward the sky.

This scene wasn't one where fire erupted, and then flew. Light was all we saw.

An orange spot, artificial, toxic, trembled as the column of smoke lifted it up and away. I was able to sense that an immensely heavy object was being forced into the sky.

"Soaring" wasn't the right word; it wasn't sleek at all. Violently, it thrust up. Its mass hammered from the bottom every few milliseconds, a giant heap of metal was being driven deep into the heavens.

Earth's gravity persisted in trying to drag it down.

Defying that force was a real struggle.

If the mass lost power for even an instant, an invisible hand would seize it and yank it all the way back.

What was unfolding was nothing but the phenomenon of a powerful, violent force pushing an object upwards.

I watched the fierce battle between human ingenuity and the laws of nature.

A tower was rising, carrying a trembling light into the sky.

The light pierced the clouds, and its tail grew.

Flames scorched the clouds.

The smoke drew an arch in the sky—the mobile nozzle had changed pitch. The SSB must have burned out a while back, and the SRB-As had detached as well.

Fiery smoke roasted the air, kicked it down again and again.

Sound struck the air, which then slapped another layer of atmosphere, serially.

A rising column.

Beyond the sea.

Beyond the windmill.

The orange light kept shoving dense smoke down onto the terrain.

Rocked by terrifying vibrations, the artificial object leapt into the darkness.

A tiny, violent mass had departed from the small island called Earth.

For a split second, a worry crossed my mind: *What if the launch fails? What if it explodes as I watch?*

In that ominous thought, I found a small wish: *May the launch fail*...and was immensely disturbed.

Fall, dammit.

The wish existed in me unceremoniously, yet clearly, like graffiti in a classroom corner.

As I watched the light shine through the thin clouds, however, the wish retreated and vanished without a trace.

The light escaped Earth and was no longer visible.

The column of smoke cast a straight shadow across the ground.

Teased by the wind, the contrails flopped over and ceased to be a column.

The first clump of smoke released at takeoff had spread over the ground and was now rising like a cumulonimbus cloud.

The wind blew all around us.

The grass swayed.

Silence.

A lingering moment.

Kanae and I stood next to each other, gazing up wordlessly.

We let out a breath at the same time.

I could finally hear the sound of waves in the distance.

The white smoke that the rocket left behind looked just like a snake, swelling, twisting, yet still slithering upwards.

A twittering bird flew between us.

The slanted light of the evening sun.

The smoke surged, then grew gradually thinner as it spread itself out.

We stood still and kept staring at the fading line of smoke.

I don't want you to fly.

When that final, impure regret vanished, all of the noise echoing in me withdrew and disappeared as well. I knew that the last hook connecting me to the "here and now" had lost its grip. All of my senses intensified. I could tell: I had been rebuilt as a thing that forges straight ahead.

I wasn't the same person that I'd been before the launch.

That rocket was me.

I didn't have to stay.

1

That night. I had a dream.

From a hilltop, I am watching the sun rise over the ocean on another planet.

A nebula floats in the gentle green sky. A small bird sings a quiet song as it flies.

Above the patterns in the sky, an otherworldly wind brushes over the vortex.

The girl is sitting on the grass, holding her knees.

She is taking in the breeze.

Just then, a light flashes across the horizon.

The orange light of a rocket, slowly ascending the boundary between the ocean and the sky...

No, I am mistaken.

What has risen is a golden sun.

A morning light enveloped in kindness...an ideal sun—only distilling beauty and silence and never burning your eyes, no matter how long you stare at it.

A swaying field of flowers.

They tremble, eager to bathe in the light.

The girl stands up. Her long hair is flowing.

Light crawls along, chasing night's shadows from the hill. Like a wave it glides toward our feet.

The light warms us from the ground up.

The girl soaks in it.

Then, she turns to face me.

Her face that was always obscured.
Her face, bathed in light, has turned towards me.
I look.
I am confused.
"Who...are you?"
I do not know.
I do not know who she is.
I reach out to her for the first time.

2

I woke up. My hand was reaching into the air, not touching anything. "Who are you?" I muttered. My voice ricocheted off the ceiling, shattered to pieces, and dissolved into thin air.

Chapter Three
5 Centimeters per Second

20

"What? What did you say just now?"

After hearing some surprising news, Akari Shinohara quickly turned around.

An easygoing person by nature, she rarely ever moved so fast.

She'd been preparing her presentation handout in the underground student lounge.

A junior majoring in Japanese Lit at a so-called private "megaversity" in Tokyo, she was twenty-one this year.

She would be taking more and more seminars as a junior and was busy skimming literary journals in search of material for her presentations. Their quality depended solely on the time and effort put into them, so unlike with tests, cramming all night didn't work.

Akari couldn't stand the thought of embarrassing herself in front of the whole class, but also enjoyed contemplating interesting pieces of literature. She made steady progress in her studies every day.

It was winter. In the lounge with its chilly vinyl flooring, she was composing a handwritten handout like always, when she overheard some unexpected news and couldn't help but ask.

"I said Sasaki in British & American Lit is getting married."

"But isn't she the same age as us?"

"Yeah, but she wants to get married ASAP. And it's not because she got knocked up or anything. She's gonna have the ceremony in

Hawaii, and then she's taking a year off from college and coming back to school the year after that, before seminars start up again."

How luxurious, one of Akari's lit-major friends chimed in enviously. Another girl, staring through the foggy window and into the winter sky, muttered that she wished she could go to Hawaii too.

"But she's barely over twenty…" Akari said, taken aback.

"So? I mean, it's surprising since she's still in school, but it's not that uncommon at our age. Pretty soon it won't be weird for us to think about. You've never thought about marriage before, Aka?"

"No, never…"

The conversation then shifted to the groom-to-be, but Akari had stopped listening.

Wow, I'm old enough to get married without it being weird. When did that happen?

It was a completely unreal idea that was oddly affecting.

She felt a bit dumbfounded.

As a kid, I never even imagined that I'd be old enough to marry one day.

The simple act of living used to terrify her beyond belief.

Life only got easier with each passing year. How funny.

For a moment, Akari reflected back on her childhood.

She used to feel convinced that no one would ever love or accept her.

She'd been absolutely sure.

Something must have happened to flip her perception of the world.

Right.

That boy had made sure she was okay.

The gas stove's quiet crackle suddenly caught Akari's attention.

I wonder how he's doing.

She began to think about the boy from her distant memories.

Hadn't she stolen something vital from him on that wintry day?

She couldn't describe it well, but something like the strength you need to survive.

Back then, they huddled together, each of them only half a person. Sharing one person's strength between the two of them, they were somehow able to live.

19

"Everyone gets frustrated when things aren't ideal, but you can't expect people to be perfect. Normal relationships should be based on realistic standards. But you're especially unforgiving in the way you try to grade me off some biased system where anything that's not perfect gets a failing mark. It's just not a fair way to judge people. Am I wrong?" Takaki Tohno said to the woman.

Takaki was twenty-one years old, and it was almost the end of winter. He studied analysis at the School of Science at his university, to which he traveled on foot from his place in Ikebukuro.

Earlier that year, he had started a part-time job as a teacher at a cram school.

There, he had fallen for a woman his age and begun a relationship that was now about to end.

She had felt special from the moment he met her.

Takaki had no trouble understanding the part of her that she carefully tucked away and that no one else ever understood.

The first time he laid his eyes on her, a tornado swept through his heart.

Nearly every bit of him seemed to spin violently, and his very sense of self got entangled in it. The noise that had accumulated in him was shredded, gone. The eye of that storm invited him in. There in the calm, under a spotlight, was the very core of her existence. He touched it.

Takaki intuited that she felt the same way about him.

They had met their other halves, as you did only once in a lifetime. They were sure of it.

Like castaways coming across fresh water, they satisfied their mutual thirst. When they couldn't meet, they missed each other so badly that their hands trembled. Their hearts shook, as if about to come undone. Takaki could feel her longing for him and knew that she felt his longing for her too.

They could sense each other's feelings almost fully—without depending on unreliable words.

For a stormy month, they craved one another.

After exactly one month, as if with calculated precision, those feelings turned into hate.

They despised each other. In the two months that followed, Takaki mastered, to a frightening degree, the art of inflicting emotional damage.

Certain approaches could cut deeper than any direct insult. Listing up things about her that she was well aware of but unable to fix, as if she weren't aware of them at all, for example.

The woman had an illness where she needed to keep her medicine on her at all times.

On a number of occasions during her bouts, Takaki had had to bring her pills and a glass of water to her lips.

The first time they made love, he was shocked to discover how skinny she was.

"You sure you're not just skin and bones?" he joked.

She made a straight face and went silent.

"I only have about half of all my organs."

"How about your brain?"

"That's the first time anyone's ever asked," she replied dryly. A relieved smile appeared on her face. "Half my organs went to my conjoined twin sister when we were separated as kids."

Takaki contemplated this for a bit. He was fairly confident in his ability to figure out people's childhoods and hadn't pegged her as someone with a twin sister.

"Really?" he asked.

She giggled. "Just kidding. I've got the full set."

They clearly hated each other but continued to date.

They just couldn't resist meeting up, one on one, fully aware that they'd be hurling hurtful words at each other.

Despite all the loathing, both of them were in desperate need of a partner.

They were hoping to be babied, if only in their savage manner, as Takaki realized much later. It was when a person meant nothing at all that you could go ahead and be totally generous.

However, neither of them could withstand such torture yet.

For Takaki, finding flaws in her was like child's play.

They were simply the traits he didn't want to accept in himself.

He just had to hide his ugliness and foist it on her.

On the day he decided against ever meeting her again, he tried a line he'd kept in reserve until then.

"By the way, where's your twin sister now?"

"...Do I have to know?"

It was snowing.

18

After studying for the entrance exams for months and months, Akari Shinohara managed to pass them and to become a college freshman when she was nineteen. In other words, she got in on her first try.

She went through the university's front gates, which were flanked by large cherry trees, for her proverbial passage under the blossoms.

Tiny petals, almost pure white, were fluttering down.

Ahh, freedom.

Akari was ecstatic.

She had spent an entire year serving the banner of "entrance exams" and put off many things.

For the very first time, she rented an apartment and started living on her own. It had been her dream.

Although they quarreled about it, her mother knew that commuting every day from Iwafune, Tochigi, to Tokyo was impossible, and eventually gave in.

Akari was fairly pleased with her apartment. The building was made of wood but clean inside to appeal to female college students. Her unit featured what qualified as a bay window, and the door had more than one lock. It was even close enough to walk to school.

Sometimes she cooked for herself; sometimes she just skipped a meal. She woke up and went to bed when she pleased, without anyone telling her what to do. She found the whole experience incredibly enjoyable.

Speaking of enjoyable, she bought herself a full set of applicators and tried wearing real makeup for the first time.

Even she had to admit, though, that her overeager attempt came out awful.

She looked better not wearing any. Removing all of it, she sulked all the way to college.

That day she realized she could tell who the freshmen girls were from how well they dolled themselves up. Looking around, she noticed that the newcomers had given themselves similar, amateurish makeup jobs. It was kind of funny.

She found classrooms with unassigned seating and long ninety-minute lectures refreshing.

She was nervous in this new environment, of course, but it no longer made her tremble or feel sick like in the past.

She made friends without a hitch.

She never had trouble finding lunch partners.

Nor did she get anxious if she wasn't with someone 24/7. She could have fun all by herself.

To put it simply, Akari felt fulfilled.

Her closest friend at school was a girl named Nomiya. Though a knockout with a dispassionate gaze and the figure of a model, she took big, strong steps around campus, spoke like a member of the *yakuza*, and wasn't afraid to curse out any boy who dared to approach her. Akari admired all these traits the moment she saw her.

I have to become her friend.

She followed Nomiya around until they became friends. Akari was pleasantly surprised with herself; her childhood self would never have done that.

About a year after starting college, she was passionately pursued by a guy from her entering class, and he became her first real boyfriend. Although he was interesting and generally fun to be around, their relationship ended after just half a year.

I just can't say no when someone tells me they love me...

She became aware of this side of her.

When someone confessed his feelings for her, she'd think, *What?! But I don't love you at all!* Soon, however, she'd want to consider it at least.

She seemed to be wired that way. The guy had bothered to tell her, and it would be such a waste. Essentially, she suspected, she was being like a hoarder.

In this regard, Akari was the exact opposite of the guy-like Nomiya, who gruffly rejected any boy she didn't like.

"But Shino, you're also not as girly as you seem," Nomiya observed. She'd taken to calling Akari by the first character of her family name.

"You think?"

"With you, looks are deceiving. You act like a girly-girl but are as straight as an arrow."

"It's like archery for me?"

"No, no, you're trying to get as close to your ideal self as possible, like an ascetic. You probably don't even know you're doing it."

"You sure about that?" Though Akari tilted her head, Nomiya's words seemed to brush against some memory.

"Water world. The world is sinking."

Nomiya was the type to say strange things out of the blue.

"What now?"

"Well, there's two kinds of people. People who start swimming in a hustle to reach some sorta destination, and people who're good just floating there peacefully. Being at a college, that became so clear to me. You're obviously a swimmer, Shino."

"Such a simple way to label people…"

While it was appallingly crude, the classification scheme made some sense to Akari, and she found herself humming lightly in assent.

"I have to make it simple or else it'd be too hard to explain. You can split the groups, of course. Hell, there's two kinds of floaters: those who are chillin', thinking they're at a hot springs, and those who're struggling with weights around their ankles. So all things considered, I think you and I have got it pretty good. In terms of where we are, that is."

Akari thought so too. At least, she didn't have to struggle to keep things the way they were.

"By the way, there's also two kind of swimmers."

"Okay, okay, I'll bite. What are they like?"

"Some know where they're going and are swimming to their destination, while others are blindly flailing in the water, trying to figure out where to go. If the swimmers with destinations overdo it, though, they're pretty much the same as the floaters being dragged down by weights. Their goals are different, but not their actions."

"Huh…you really think so?"

"Our world seems to link into a circle. It's a Ringworld."

In hindsight, this might have been Nomiya's way of warning Akari, who was in love at the time. Seriously in love—to put it mildly.

The winter rain was pouring down.

It wasn't because Akari had heard her acquaintance was getting married—but unwilling to feel driven by a game of association, she at least made sure to wait for a while before slowly making her way out of the lounge.

She went through an outside corridor to another building on campus. When the cold air hit her, she could feel the chilly moisture seep into her hair.

The offices of the British & American Literature professors lined the hallway. She saw that the lights were on in the room she was headed to, and the jolt that ran through her body felt almost magnetic.

Since there was no answer when she knocked, she cracked open the door.

The professor's eyes didn't leave his PC.

"Excuse me, may I come in?"

"As long as you don't speak while I work."

A tight, painful feeling seized her chest, but Akari took a deep breath and sat at the small sofa suite in front of his desk.

The man continued typing away on his keyboard, not pausing even for a moment to think.

She pictured the big hands hiding behind the monitor.

The university allowed students to earn general-education credits for taking a different department's core courses.

As a sophomore, Akari had taken The History of British & American Literature, an introductory course, and a seminar in translation. Seated before her was the instructor of those classes.

More renowned as a translator than a scholar, he had a beautiful writing style. That was the initial reason Akari signed up for his classes.

Soon enough, however, she began to have a different reason.

The man, who completely ignored her as if she were nothing but air as he worked, gave off a unique vibe, for instance in how he would crane his neck.

The only way she could put it was that she loved it.

There was no clear reason as to why.

If she knew why she loved him, she might have quit him for good. Persuading herself that it was a bad reason would be the end of it.

Without a reason, however, she was stuck on him.

Without a reason, she suffered.

It was all in her head, so why couldn't she stop?

Come to think of it, though, you could never explain why you fell in love.

Some things could be described in words, but not others.

Naming the reason you loved someone was a prime example of the latter.

She seriously questioned all those magazine surveys that claimed "kindness" was the most desirable quality in the opposite sex.

Akane, at least, had never fallen for a "kind" man. Not even once.

She didn't think those surveys were fake. The majority of women must have answered that way, of course.

Yet she doubted they had ever fallen for a guy because he was kind. He might have turned out to be kind.

The respondents had to be falling in love for reasons they couldn't even understand or describe, and just replying "a kind man" because it was the safest option.

That was probably it.

If not, then—

"Okay, do you have any questions for me?"

The man's hand made little waving motions, but not to greet Akari. He was just relaxing his muscles after tearing his hand away from the keyboard.

"Not really…"

"Then why did you come?"

"I can't stop by without a proper reason?"

"That would be a waste of time, for both of us."

Why did she feel so deeply for him when he wasn't kind, let alone interested in her?

She took care to sound as calm as possible. "I find it hard to believe that you're too busy even to chat for a little while."

"If I take the concentration I am using on this conversation and direct it somewhere else, I might have another brilliant insight. Anything that robs me of that possibility has to be seen as a waste of time. It's not a novel concept, you know. Maybe one day you'll understand."

"May I ask you a question then?"

"Answering questions is part of my job."

"Have you thought about us since then?"

His expression remained unchanged.

"Honestly, not at all."

"Aren't you single, professor?"

"That is a private matter, but, yes, I am."

"I heard you're not currently seeing anyone."

"That is also private information, but, yes, that is true."

"Hypothetically, you might develop an interest in me due to our time together outside of class. What are your thoughts on that?"

"It's possible, sure. However, I've already decided not to let it get to that point. I should be dedicating that time to other matters instead."

Akari couldn't help but sigh. It was a painful exhalation that made her lungs itch. "Now I know what it feels like to want to ask, 'Which is more important for you, love or work?'"

"That's merely a question of what interests you more at a given time. No proper answer exists. There will be cases where I am more interested in my work, and cases where I don't find the partner all that interesting."

"What is it that interests you so much?"

"Gathering data, fully analyzing it, and creating new information. Through that process I can heighten my skills."

"How do other people fit into that process?"

"They don't, in my case."

"Well, then what makes you happy?"

"I don't live to find happiness. Those who do live empty lives. A goal needs to be more specific."

"So, your goal isn't to be happy?"

"Right."

"And you plan to live that way forever?"

"Correct."

"I don't think anyone can sympathize with that."

"Giving or receiving sympathy is meaningless."

"What?"

"I don't think anyone's sympathy is worth anything. Logical argumentation and the absolute value it can return are what's universal."

Alone, and feeling out of it, Akari entered a café along a boulevard.

She took her coffee black, unlike always. She wanted the bitter taste to counteract the bitterness in her heart.

"I don't need you in my life."

In the end, that was what the instructor meant.

It was the first time she'd been told such a thing, and so directly too.

Well, maybe not the first time...

Akari's past was lousy with rejection, even if it hadn't been put into words. There'd been such a phase in her life.

She rested her elbows on the table.

She put her hands to her forehead.

Her umbrella, which she had propped against her chair, promptly slid to the floor.

She felt doomed to a life of unrequited love.

A melancholy song in triple meter suddenly began playing on the USEN radio. Akari knew the song. It was "First Love" by Mayumi Kojima. It was exactly the kind of song she didn't want to hear.

She wanted to get up and leave, but didn't have the strength.

It was the worst feeling imaginable.

I miss you, she thought.

Whom did she miss?

I don't know.

17

After a belated job hunt, Takaki somehow secured an entry position. It was already the end of autumn.

A professor of his had managed to land him a job at a software development company in Mitaka City. The firm turned a profit by receiving orders, designing programs, and manufacturing and delivering the product.

Takaki became a so-called systems engineer. In the narrow sense of the word, this meant working in both systems design and marketing, but he also coded because the projects were small in scale.

While the mid-sized company was not a household name, it was on a growth path and highly regarded in the industry. Everyone said he was "lucky" for finding a way into the company.

And Takaki knew it, too. He was fortunate.

Because there he learned that it was programming that suited him most.

Having used a computer for his research in college, he understood the basics. At the company, however, he came to believe that the field had been made for him.

"Lucky" was the only way to describe his chance meeting with his vocation.

He could immerse himself in his monitor behind the walls of his cubicle, take care of entire meetings just through email, and not waste time on monotonous small talk with his fellow employees—he liked it for those antisocial reasons too.

But what was moving to him was that a functioning framework emerged when he tirelessly piled one "description" upon another and compiled those scripts.

He never would have guessed that he was so suited to engineering.

He buried himself in a box.

His very existence was being transferred into the sequences of code he created.

When he tore off pieces of himself and packed them in the box, they began to function, to multiply, and to work on their own.

He was getting drunk off that cycle.

The computer on his desk seemed to exist in its own independent world. Beyond his monitor was an alternate universe that had different laws from reality.

He reached into that universe and rearranged its contents to his liking. Through sheer willpower and hard work, he could give life to things that had never existed before.

Before he was even aware of it, he started thinking of his job as building a tower on an empty field. Sometimes he imagined that he was creating fictional animals.

He could bring things to life.

The next time, he would make something bigger.

It was exhilarating, the pleasure and satisfaction of mastering a new skill.

Come up with an idea.

Make it a reality.

Refine yourself through that process.

The future seemed so bright.

He was proud of his creations.

He was making rapid progress and wasn't going to stop. He was moving forward.

Amidst the daily repetition, that got him high.

Higher.

He wanted to go higher.

A couple of years flew by while he was steeped in that notion.

Before he knew it, he had become one of the most proficient employees at his company.

While that fact brought him joy, he could sense the noise mounting around him. He tried his hardest to shake it off, to ignore it, but it was simply no use.

More and more often, a company bottleneck prevented him from moving up. Being dragged down by his less skilled colleagues was excruciating.

He tried to reach higher, but a ceiling blocked him, and there were weights around his ankles.

It was oppressive and suffocating.

Nothing frustrated Takaki more than unmotivated employees and stalled projects.

He learned something: the more incompetent the workers, the more they tended to deny that they were deadweight. In the end, that was what ineptitude meant.

He was stuck behind a runner who was behind an entire lap.

Get going.

What do you even live for?

At least don't hold me back...

"Some people are scared to take the shortest path."

That was what Risa Mizuno said, with a soft sigh, on one of the rare occasions Takaki opened up to her about his workplace irritations.

"Most people purposely take the long road. They prefer to take their time understanding things, dwelling on how tired their legs feel. A lot of people just can't accept what others tell them even if it's true, and won't be convinced of anything unless they noticed it themselves. That's just the way things are."

After she gently reproached him, the tension went out of him, and he felt much better.

Risa's voice and words seemed to have that mysterious effect. Upon returning to work, of course, various things would irritate him all over again.

Still, Takaki wondered why there was a touch of sadness in her face when she spoke that way.

"Mr. Tohno—from Systems, right?"

That was how Risa approached Takaki on a platform in Shinjuku Station. He would later look back on it as being quite uncharacteristic of her.

In his estimation, she wasn't the type to accost a mere acquaintance on the street.

"Uh...yes?" he answered, somewhat taken aback.

He assumed only pollsters or salespeople ever approached him on the street, so he was surprised to hear someone mention his last name and company.

It took him a few seconds to remember who she was.

That small lapse of time was just long enough to make Takaki miss his train. He was simply heading home after seeing a movie, though.

Risa worked at a client company of Takaki's and was the assistant of the man who handled his account.

The only interaction Risa and Takaki had ever had was at a brief meeting where they had exchanged business cards.

Takaki could never go up to someone he barely knew on the street. Her calm manner of approaching him piqued his interest.

While perhaps sexist, he also thought it was rare for a young woman to spend her free time wandering the streets of Shinjuku alone on a weekend.

He politely invited her to join him for tea, and Risa accepted with a nod and a smile.

That smile was still burned on the back of his mind.

They left through the east exit and talked over tea for two hours at the Omokage Café.

There wasn't a single pause in their conversation the entire time.

Takaki thought it might be the longest he'd ever been absorbed in any conversation.

They spoke with great passion.

They had the same opinion on many topics. While they didn't always see eye to eye, Takaki respected Risa's logical, well-grounded takes even when he didn't fully agree with her.

She was thoughtful and responsive. It had been ages since he had shared his views like that.

He'd wanted to talk to someone but never realized it.

That, or he'd been trying to convince himself that he didn't want to talk to anyone at all.

Takaki talked until his throat hurt. He used to think that "talking your throat sore" was an unrealistic lie invented by celebrities to brag about how much they spoke, but now he knew that it could actually happen.

All it had taken to get him to talk was someone who understood him.

It was the most fulfilling, refreshing, and fun couple of hours he had enjoyed in a number of years, or so he felt.

There was one development that troubled him, though.

Takaki was playing a guessing game about Risa.

"If you think you can guess correctly, by all means," she assented playfully. She most likely underestimated his intuition.

He silently gazed at the woman, who looked quite lovely in her glasses as she played with her straw across the table.

Takaki had a knack for telling if a person had siblings even if they had just met. Just from talking, he could also guess, eight times out of ten, whether someone was the eldest or youngest child, and whether there were any siblings of the opposite sex.

No older sister.

No younger sister, either. She doesn't seem like she was raised with another girl around her age.

No younger brother, given the way she's interacting with me, a guy.

"If you're not an only child, you have a brother who's a lot older than you."

It was a shot in the dark, but the moment he said it she became visibly upset. He seemed to have infringed on some serious private matter.

Risa tried to hide her distress, and she did so quite well, one might say. Takaki, however, was too accustomed to seeing through such facades.

He judged her to be the type who concealed various secrets beneath the surface.

"…Correct," Risa replied, faking a smile.

She didn't say which of his statements.

"I'm guessing you're a people person?" she asked.

Takaki just smiled. It was the exact opposite. He was neither interested in nor attached to any individual, which was why he fitted them into patterns.

Yet he took a strong interest in Risa, a woman he had only invited to tea on a whim, once he identified with her *aura of trying to hide something*.

It seemed like she was desperately averting her own eyes.

Perhaps it aroused in him a sense of solidarity.

They exchanged phone numbers and email addresses. Since then, they started meeting up almost every week.

"I would really like to see your place," Takaki said after one of their several dates.

"Sure," Risa agreed.

16

Her apartment was as neat as a showroom.

She seemed to be trying to keep her furniture to a minimum, which made her medium-sized room look rather large.

While he could only guess at the time, she also seemed to have crammed all of her sundries behind the louver doors of her walk-in closet.

The walls were white, and all of the furniture and fittings were made of wood. The walnut-colored flooring was properly waxed, and the kitchen was sparkling clean despite regular use.

Risa cooked her own meals every day, as Takaki learned later. It was more of a "ritual" than a routine.

He could see that she put a lot of effort into organizing her space. *This is the total opposite of my sloppy lifestyle*, he thought.

While the bureau, chairs, and bed were antiques, she did not own a sofa or low table. In other words, she hadn't expected guests when she had set up her room.

After Takaki started making frequent visits, she bought a low table and cushions.

He liked the looks of her place. A room is very telling about one's temperament, after all, and hers gave him a positive impression. He found her place quite cozy.

During his first visit, he suddenly wanted to see how it might feel working there.

"Would you mind if I worked a bit?" he asked, taking out his laptop.

She seemed surprised, a little angry, and quite disgusted. After that rush of emotions, a resigned expression appeared on her face.

"Fine, go ahead," she said rather halfheartedly.

Watching Takaki happily type away on his keyboard, however, seemed to improve her mood.

Takaki never felt more relaxed working than the brief time he did so in Risa's apartment. He rarely ever hummed as contentedly as he did that day.

"But I'm surprised. I still can't believe it."

It was after they had slept together on a few occasions that she said this.

"For the longest time, I thought no one would ever love me. I never imagined I'd be able to touch or be touched by someone like this. I always thought I'd live my whole life unloved."

"Looks like you were wrong."

"Can I touch you a little more?"

The nervous way she stroked his cheek felt so new to him, but also evoked a strange sense of déjà vu.

"Your body heat is so calming. How your bones feel, too."

Same here.

A fleeting flashback that vanished almost as soon as it came made him concur.

Risa was stunned by the chaotic state of his room.

"Can I tidy it up a bit?" she requested.

"No."

Somehow, over the years, Takaki had lost the ability to keep his space clutter-free.

He found the process of putting each and every object back in its assigned position a complete waste of time. If anyone ever cleaned up his place, he probably wouldn't be able to find a thing.

"Why do you have this stuff?" Risa asked from the kitchen.

It was tidy there, only because it went unused. She was holding a pair of scissors in her right hand and a Yakishime tea cup in her left.

She seemed puzzled as to why he owned such high-quality kitchenware when he didn't even cook.

"Ahh, those. They're from Tanegashima."

There was a brand-new knife from Tanegashima under the sink, but he had never used it. He had brought it with him when he moved to Tokyo.

"I lived in Tanegashima until I graduated high school."

"Tanegashima? The place famous for having the first guns in Japan?"

"Right, the one with the guns."

"I didn't know you were raised on an island, Takaki. You don't give off an 'island vibe' at all."

"Well, I didn't really grow up there. I moved there when I was in my second year of junior high. But they make really nice blades on the island, so I guess I'm spoiled in that department."

"Tanegashima's in Kagoshima, right?"

"Right."

"You don't seem like someone from the southern islands. Just judging from your image, that is."

"What's my 'image'?"

"Somewhere more up north. Where it snows."

Takaki smiled. Risa handed him the cup, which he then placed on a plate on the table. The water on the stove still needed a bit more time to boil.

"Tanegashima is red, just like this cup."

"Red? How?"

"It's the soil."

"Huh?"

"All of the soil on the island. The soil's red for the same reason blood is: there's tons of iron in the ground. That's why all of Tanegashima's pottery is red. The island used to be a major steel producer back in the day. Actually, I think it still is."

"And they also make knives there?"

"Yeah. Never heard of Tanegashima knives? They're really famous."

"Can't say I have."

"They even used to call muskets 'Tanegashimas,' but the fact that the first ones were brought there isn't the real reason. It's actually because Tanegashima used to be a major producer of them."

Takaki felt a bit sentimental as he spoke.

Looking back on it now, life on the island really wasn't so bad.

Not that thinking so now changed a thing.

Risa slept over that night. Listening to her breathe in her sleep, with her forehead nudged against his shoulder, he found it all quite strange.

A defenseless woman was sleeping beside him. He had never really imagined this situation.

He had been in a few relationships, but no one had ever been quite like this.

Risa completely let her guard down.

She left herself so vulnerable that Takaki wondered if she was okay.

He didn't know people could let others in as much as she let him in.

He was astonished.

No one had ever slept next to him so peacefully in all his life.

Her breathing sounded like the ebbing tide.

For a short while, Takaki enjoyed the nostalgic illusion of being enveloped by that island's air.

15

To put it mildly, Akari had a very tough time finding a job.

It was a time when the economy was said to be in a ten-year recession, and it seemed like every company had become extra selective in hiring new graduates. The winds of change were especially chilly to girls who had studied literature and didn't have any special skills.

The professors and the mood around her had warned her how tough it would be to get a job, so she had at least been prepared. She ran around, going from orientation session to interview, and applied to every job that she could.

Who ever said that "college is a four-year moratorium"?

Akari had never been so exhausted in her life. Passing the college entrance exam was a thousand times easier than finding a job.

Eventually, a bookstore chain with large outlets in Tokyo hired her.

The company wasn't the number one leader in its industry but an adequate enterprise that competed for the number two or three spot.

At first, Akari worked as a shop clerk. Surrounded by thousands of books every day, she felt that her workplace was close to ideal.

By the time she had gotten used to folding book covers, organizing the bookshelves, using the cash register, and interacting with customers, she found that a year had flown by.

After two years at an outlet, her request to move to a different department was approved, and she promptly began training to become a buyer.

She didn't just work with books because she loved them, she also wanted to try selling them as a proper form of business.

She started perusing weekly, gossip, and boys' magazines, and through genres of books she did not care for at all.

She put her personal preferences aside and thought about these items' market appeal. She also thought about the people who needed them.

After she made some terrible slip-ups and was harshly reprimanded, she couldn't get back on her feet for quite some time.

Nevertheless, her love for books and reading never waned.

Her work wasn't all fun and games, but it was fun just the same.

She was simply happy to work with books and to be surrounded by them in her workplace. Sending her favorites out into the world brought her great joy.

After Akari transferred departments, her network grew significantly.

In-store, she had dealt with "the general public," but after going into purchasing she began to handle a lot more "people who have names and faces."

In that sense, her current post actually expanded her horizons.

She also met someone after becoming a buyer. He was a sales rep for a publisher.

As a member of the working world, Akari had noticed that nearly all salespeople exuded a certain unique energy.

She figured it was because being assertive and bluffing was essential to their job.

It seemed that many salesmen donned the image of being a "go-getter" like armor. While she didn't work in sales herself, she worried that it must really tire one out.

"It's exhausting, it really is," the man admitted. "I mean, the whole salesman act isn't natural at all. I've learned the tricks of the trade and now do it without thinking, of course, but it's like a jam-packed train: even if you get used to it, it tires you out."

She found it amusing that he was the image of "Yes, I can!" when she saw him at work but was completely laid-back when they met up in private.

She also liked how he seemed to have had a good upbringing and didn't seem greedy.

He was honestly more of a goofball than she expected. It wasn't a bad thing. In fact, she was really fond of his absentmindedness.

She was glad that he wasn't stuck in business mode all the time; a guy like that would have certainly worn her out.

"I bet you do well in love, Ms. Shinohara."

He told her he imagined she'd had plenty of wonderful relationships in the past.

"Oh, that's not true."

"Well, I think it just might be."

He added that naturally she must have had some rough experiences as well.

"But I'm sure those experiences made you into the lovely person you are today. That's the feeling I get from you."

Does he honestly think that some sweet words will win me over? she thought. But being complimented like that frankly didn't feel all that bad.

14

Takaki and Risa had been dating for two years.

Since both of them had busy jobs, they always met at night. As soon as it grew dark outside his office window, Takaki thought about Risa.

They would email each other, meet somewhere to dine, and have a few drinks. That was their usual routine.

They sat at the counter of a bar in Nakano called "The Shanghai Doll," which has since shut down. Takaki always ordered whiskey, while Risa either got a brandy sour or a time warp cocktail.

"What were you like when you were young, Takaki?"

"I was a pretty average kid."

"You're joking."

"Well, I did change schools a lot."

"Because of your parents' work?"

"Yeah."

Risa glanced at the lit-up, multicolored bottles of booze. "I'm a little jealous… I always wished I could transfer schools," she murmured.

"Why's that?"

"I mean, you get a clean slate, right? You can clear your image, your reputation, everything. All I ever wanted was a second chance."

"It's a lot tougher than you think."

"How so?"

"Well, you have to make your way into fully formed relationships as an outsider."

"You know, there was this girl who transferred into my class when I was in elementary school. She was really pretty, and really, really popular. A lot of the kids envied her, but most of them really liked her."

"You never saw her let her guard down, did you?"

"Huh? Well no, probably not."

"She must've had a good head on her shoulders. Deep down, she must have always been on edge."

"Were you like that, too?"

"Maybe. I'm not sure how other people saw me."

"You weren't bullied, were you?"

"No, not really… When you change schools again and again, you kind of learn how to blend in after a while."

As they walked home side by side that night, Risa said, "I'm really shy about meeting people."

"I know."

"So I wonder why I felt so calm with you from the beginning." Hooking arms with Takaki, she leaned her upper body against him. "Oh, what am I going to do? I really love you, Takaki."

He could only respond with an embarrassed smile. Despite the scent of her skin, and her hair brushing his neck, he kept walking, his eyes focused straight ahead.

His embarrassed smile was just a pretense.

He should have said, "I love you, too."

For some reason he couldn't.

Something was up with Risa. Takaki sensed it the very first time he met her, and the impression stayed with him.

What was burdening her revealed itself without warning.

Late one night at Takaki's apartment, she began sobbing in her sleep like a little child. He woke with a start.

"What's wrong?"

He turned over in bed and touched her shoulder. As if that had activated some kind of switch, she curled herself into a ball and screwed up her face as she cried.

"I had a dream about my older brother. He was standing on the train platform," she squeezed out breathlessly between her hysterical sobs.

Takaki sat up and gazed down at her. She had pulled the covers close and wrapped her arms around herself as though to suppress her convulsions.

Her big brother?

Takaki went into the kitchen and fetched her some cold mineral water. He sat her up, but she couldn't even gulp down the water.

Takaki just watched in silence. What else could he do?

For a long time, she continued to take small hiccups of breath.

He didn't ask anything.

With her hand against her forehead, Risa unexpectedly began to speak in a trembling voice, between trembling exhalations. She was talking to herself more or less, and there were many parts Takaki couldn't comprehend, but he came to understand a few things.

When Risa was in her second year of junior high, her older brother had jumped off the platform, into an oncoming train.

It was assumed to be suicide.

"After that...it was all over, everything went to hell..."

The gears powering her went out of whack. Abruptly, the circuits that had helped her "get along" with her peers and navigate her environment fell apart.

From that point on, she had trouble fitting in wherever she was.

She talked about the bitter loneliness of school. About the days when no one would look at her.

Just listening to her trembling voice recount all this froze Takaki to the core.

He recalled what a coworker of his, Hasegawa, had once told him: the death of an older brother means something different to his younger siblings compared to any other death in the family.

Since Hasegawa worked in human resources, he consoled employees when they were bereaved. Through that experience, he had noticed that among the deaths of siblings, an older brother's was the most damaging.

Sometimes employees suffering a death in the family had trouble getting back on their feet to the point that their work suffered. More often than not, in those cases, the deceased wasn't a parent, sister, or younger brother, but an older brother.

Takaki didn't have any siblings and had taken Hasegawa's word for it—or rather, hadn't felt entirely convinced. Wouldn't the level of suffering be the same no matter which sibling passed away?

But now, Takaki suspected that his colleague was right.

According to Hasegawa, an older brother was probably closer to his siblings than their parents and a bigger role model. He was tasked with balancing out the family.

Risa was weeping bitterly in the fetal position, her chest still shaking.

With every experience of a loved one's death, the survivor settled deeper into reality. As if gravity had strengthened by that much.

Takaki was mature enough to understand that. He thought back on the deaths of a few people he'd known. It felt like he'd taken on a little more weight again.

He remained silent, unable to speak.

The fluorescent lights' white noise droned in his ears and numbed his head.

Risa was crying her eyes out because of a dream she had about her older brother.

He couldn't do anything.

He did know what to do. He needed to cradle her head in his arms and tell her she was going to be okay. He really ought to have. That simple act would have alleviated her pain.

Why couldn't he do that much?

And what was it that her brother had found beyond the platform?

13

The next time Takaki met with Risa, she behaved like none of it had ever happened. If she was suffering inside, she appeared unfazed on the surface.

Seeing this, he pretended not to have seen nor heard anything that night and just spoke to her normally. The only difference was that he was gentler when he reached out to touch her.

He was busier with work than ever before.

On top of being skilled he was passionate, so he naturally received outstanding evaluations. As thanks he got assigned to some other stalled project that needed him, and the cycle continued.

Without complaining, he burrowed through as if he were a drill digging a new metro tunnel.

Eventually, he got stuck with the much-feared "slowest moving" project in the company.

Initiated before Takaki ever joined the developer, no one knew where it was going or when it would end.

It was like digging a hole to fill up another hole. The goal was to create flat ground, but it seemed entirely impossible.

Takaki untiringly chipped away at it.

"So damn heavy…" he muttered.

He was referring to the program he was processing, but his words shot through his body.

His body felt heavy.

He picked up the paper Starbucks cup and drank from it. He couldn't taste anything.

He reclined in his chair and straightened his back.

Oops, Takaki thought.

It's not mental or physical fatigue, so what is it?

He stared up at the white ceiling—carelessly enough. His neck tendons strained.

What is this…

He searched for the right word.

"So damn painful…" he muttered.

Yes. Right answer.

Why is it so painful?

He shut his eyes. He took deep breaths.

Then he tried to sense his surroundings.

Around just him, gravity felt a lot heavier than one g…

What planet was this?

It was only going to keep getting heavier.

He could feel it.

He wouldn't be able to move…

He was getting tied down, for sure.

I see. I'm starting to get pinned down, and it's painful.

To where?

To here.

Right. He hadn't noticed. Or he'd been pretending not to notice.

He felt like he was being forced to decelerate here.

He'd become much faster than this place a good while ago.

Everything around him was too heavy, too slow.

If he didn't escape now, he wouldn't be able to get out.

He needed to escape as soon as he could.

He forced his eyes open. He knew this place was no good for him. He was in a swamp. If he didn't drag his legs forward, he would sink.

This was bad.

If he didn't wrap the project up soon, he would never be able to swim his way out.

The program had the wrong victory conditions. Its destination was wrong. It needed to be reset and downsized so its vectors could be aligned. Multiple engines were revving in different directions, and their force didn't have a central axis.

Takaki began typing ferociously, and in just half a day he completed a drastic revision plan. He may have been overstepping his duties, but he had no other choice. He ran the program using the new methodology.

He submitted the comparative data to his immediate superior.

Takaki explained that their previous method would get them nowhere.

Their efforts would simply stall and disintegrate in midair.

Perhaps he didn't use the right words. His proposal was flat-out rejected.

This was no joke. It drove Takaki crazy to know that he was aboard a sinking vessel.

He could either plug the leaks and rush to his destination before it sank, or just jump ship.

He figured that he would be better off swimming.

He went one rung higher in the company and met with the director of operations, to whom he submitted the same proposal for a change in policy.

The man's answer was blunt: just do your work and don't cause any trouble.

Takaki stubbornly experimented with his own method, created data that compared efficiency levels, and submitted his findings to a few other bosses. He didn't receive positive responses.

It was hopeless.

"Please make your decision."

Takaki's face was expressionless when he uttered those words to the director of operations one day.

The man could either revise the policy or take Takaki off the project. If the director refused to pick either option, Takaki would quit.

It was a threat that was understood as such. They took issue with his maneuver, but the executives discussed the matter and eventually decided to adopt Takaki's plan.

He was a bit relieved that some of the brass could make a logical decision. Without them, Takaki would have quit without a trace of remorse.

The superior who initially rejected his plan was transferred to a different department.

The entire project team was placed under Takaki, for all intents and purposes. He held several meetings and started taking the project forward at a previously unthinkable speed.

That was deeply satisfying.

But only at the beginning. Having forced out his own boss, Takaki had drawn his workplace in towards himself. He needed to take responsibility. It made sense, and he'd expected as much.

Files of all sorts started to pile onto his desk. Responsibilities he had never handled before began to hang over his head.

For example, he'd never had to make a group of people with different personalities work as a team.

As self-centered as it sounded, he found dealing with their quirks extremely annoying. He had to calibrate their relationships, fill out approval forms, and handle other busywork...

Meanwhile, it was a marvel how the project accelerated, and kept on accelerating. The company seemed extremely satisfied. Every time Takaki turned in one of the project's progress reports, upper management showered him with compliments, saying that he was doing a fantastic job and that he had been right all along.

Yet…

Tons of deadweight now hung off Takaki, and he was losing speed.

He tried imagining that the weight wasn't there.

He didn't want to accept that he was slow.

While the tiresome chores only mounted, he refused to reduce the daily workload he'd set for himself.

When he visited Risa, often he would just work there.

On a few occasions he kept going for hours, forgetting her presence, before panicking and asking her about her day.

Looking back on it now, perhaps he totally lacked the capacity to appreciate those little everyday things.

He hardly ever complained to Risa about work.

The first time he ever did, she had urged him to:

"Even if you don't want to talk about it, you really should."

Why was she insisting? Talking about it wasn't going to fix anything.

Letting it all out might make him feel better, and even if it didn't, the listener could pretend to get it and relax—he understood how that system worked.

But Takaki didn't think that way.

"Why don't you try a little harder to show how you feel?" she said.

If I look happy, people can feel at ease. If I look unhappy, people can worry.

In other words, it sounded like it was everyone else's problem.

Not his.

It wasn't his interiority, but that of others around him that was at issue in the proposition, "Takaki Tohno should try to show his feelings." Frankly, he couldn't care less.

If they'd let him, he wanted to deal with his emotions himself.

"I think I get it now," Risa said.

"What?"

"You told me once that changing schools didn't faze you at all."

"Right."

"You pretty much blended in with your surroundings."

"Uh huh."

"Was that because you didn't mind being misunderstood?"

She's probably right, Takaki thought.

It was easy pretending to be a wonderful person if someone didn't matter to him.

"There's only a scent," Risa said.

All that's left, she went on mumbling to herself, *is the scent of something important, something vital, in you. Someone took it away. That's why all I can hear is my sigh echoing in an empty treasure chest.*

Late into the night, Takaki dreamed about his childhood.

It was a miserable dream where the kids in class were put into teams, but only he was left out.

He woke up feeling sad. It felt like a paintbrush was grazing against his heart. Had that occurred in real life? He couldn't remember.

...Actually, that definitely happened when he was young, back when he was very young.

As Takaki washed his face—and drank some of the tap water, which faintly smelled of chlorine, while he was at it—a thought crossed his mind.

I wonder if that's ever happened to Risa.

It must have.

He was almost positive.

"Why are you asking me that?"

She would make a sad face and probably say that if he did ask her. He could picture it vividly, down to the tone of her voice.

He was quickly figuring everything out about her.

It was only natural in a serious relationship.

You understand your partner, and your partner understands you.

Phrases he once heard Risa mumbling to herself entered his head out of the blue.

Someone took it away.

An empty treasure chest.

His past, which he had sealed away at the bottom of his memory, was being excavated.

Fear.

Why?

Not knowing was what scared him.

"I don't want to stay here," his reflection in the bathroom mirror said.

Assuming any mass in someone else was something he wanted to avoid.

The guy in the mirror spoke again.

"I want to go somewhere…"

He went out in the middle of the night. There were still a few hours left until morning. He walked through the residential area, the streetlamps his only source of light. There weren't any stars.

For a moment, he was confused why the streets were odorless.

Why was there no smell?

Why didn't he smell a blend of green leaves and sea and dirt in the wind?

Well, duh. This was Tokyo.

Takaki felt terribly off-balance.

He came to a boulevard. There, he hailed a cab and headed to his office.

He went through security, inputting the passcode at the back entrance. His coworkers liked to boast that "the company never slept," but no one was there at that hour.

Switching on just the fluorescent lights above his workspace on the dark, empty floor, he started up his computer and began typing furiously, his face gleaming blue from the monitor's backlight. He typed so fast that he startled himself. He was getting drunk off the pace and the rhythm of his fingers. *Faster*, urged something in him. *Hurry up.*

If he didn't, it was going to get him.

A hand would reach for his shoulder.

Unless he was running fast, it was scary.

He didn't know what he was afraid of, but knew that he needed to run faster, farther.

But the farther he ran, the more entangled his body became.

The more wind resistance he faced.

It was trying to knock him down.

Failure was proof of weakness.

He couldn't tolerate such weakness.

He had to be strong.

And always be okay.

12

He was being tied down. He wasn't made to handle that.

Since he was falling behind at work, he would go to the office early in the morning and leave later than everyone else.

He spent less time with Risa.

He felt slowed down and exhausted at the office as usual. The friction was immense. It was like stepping on the accelerator with the handbrakes pulled.

Once the office was empty, hearing his fingers strike the keys made him want to see Risa.

That feeling, his own, felt heavy to him.

It was scary.

That he was so attached to her. The anxiety and inchoate jealousy he felt in relation to Risa Mizuno, all of the noise, was scary.

Sometimes, like now, he missed her and wanted to see her so much. For some reason, that fact was painful. He wished he could kill the emotion.

He wasn't able to see her for a couple of weeks.

When he finally went to her place for the first time in a while, she asked out of the blue, "I was thinking about buying a car. What do you think?"

"You have your driver's license?"

"Yeah, I got it when I was still a student. I thought it would be useful for job hunting."

"But why do you want a car again? The maintenance cost is such a pain."

Back when Takaki was in college, he bought a car with the money he had earned at a part-time job. It was a used Suzuki Swift that ran exceptionally well for its mileage.

He then took a solo trip around Japan. He never stayed at hotels, choosing instead to spend many nights sleeping in his car. In the end, he didn't make enough to cover the parking lot and maintenance fees and had no choice but to part with his car after just over a year.

"You know what, I'll drive you to work every morning."

"All the way there? You don't have to. I mean, it's just a train ride to my office—"

"I want to," Risa interrupted.

This was someone who always thought before she spoke, and she had never sounded so serious.

"If at all possible, I don't want you standing on a platform."

Takaki pretended not to have heard her not-so-subtle reason. "I can't let you do that. I'm already so grateful that you cook for me, and I feel bad about being busy as it is. If you drove me around on top of that, you would be my mother or something. I'm a little hesitant about it. It would be fine if I were the one driving you to work."

"Hey, it's not about how you feel, it's about what I want."

"Listen, if you want to buy a car, that's your choice. I just can't have you driving me around because I'd feel too bad about it."

Risa glanced down to her lower right and bit her bottom lip. She had the habit of doing this when she had more to say but didn't know how.

Takaki thought he did a good job of getting out of it. He felt relieved.

"I mean, is there anything I can do for you, Risa? For my part, I can't think of anything that you don't already do. Actually, I'd really like it if you were more open about what *you* want me to do."

Risa looked at Takaki with a shocked expression, as if her heart had skipped a beat.

She seemed more upset at her own thoughts than his words.

"Takaki," she said, "I have a favor to ask."

"What is it?"

"Even just once would be enough."

"Shoot."

"I want you to say it."

"Say what?"

He shouldn't have asked.

"Say that you love me."

Takaki went home. Without even turning on the lights, he opened his laptop and created a document in Microsoft Word.

It was with a half-astonished expression that he watched the display as his hands began to type up a letter of resignation.

It was probably over.

Blaming their busy schedules, Takaki and Risa spent less time together when they met.

Something had died.

He unconsciously avoided her.

Starting around October, they began to meet less often, and the months went by.

He stowed away his summer clothes and took out his winter vestments.

The season of skin-crampingly chilly nights had come around.

Takaki commuted to work wrapped tightly in his coat.

He tried not to think about how it was December 19th, Risa's birthday. He avoided the calendar at all costs. He kept averting his heart's eyes to keep it from resurfacing in his mind.

By the time Takaki had finished work, taken the train from Mitaka to Shinjuku, and slipped out of the station, the date had already changed.

Three days ago, he had completed the infamous, infuriating project. However, he still had a mountain of tasks left. He had to meet with coworkers and bosses to transition his duties over to them and say his goodbyes. He couldn't leave the office until it was this late.

He had already submitted the letter of resignation from that night.

After a month or so of attending to the tedious task of cleaning up after himself, he would finally be free of that company.

He didn't feel this way or that about it.

He just knew that he couldn't take it anymore.

Fatigue coiled around his body and weighed him down. He thought about taking a taxi to his apartment in Nakano Sakaue. He gave up on the idea 0.2 seconds after seeing the dreadful queue at the taxi stand.

The Marunouchi Line had already shut down for the night, so he decided to walk home. He didn't mind navigating the interstices of Shinjuku's skyscrapers.

When he came out on the other side of the tunnel-like west exit, the dampness of the chilly night air enveloped him.

The trees that separated the sidewalk from the street had been decorated with bluish-white lights.

It was the season. Takaki didn't really like Christmas festivities.

Still, he couldn't deny that the straight line of trees, each adorned with tiny grains of snow-like light, looked stunning in perspective. He felt the fatigue in his chest loosen up.

Takaki walked with his hands in his pockets.

His leather shoes tapped against the stone ground. The sound seemed to reverberate across the desolate district of high rises that was West Shinjuku at night.

When he approached the Sumitomo Building, a quiet buzzing came from his pocket.

Takaki stopped still, his nerves frayed by the vibration of his cell phone.

He took his paint-chipped Willcom phone in his gloved hand. A frosty wind blew. It attacked his glove and chilled his hand, which had been warm and snug in his pocket only moments ago.

He opened his flip phone. He checked his missed calls.

Risa Mizuno.

Takaki glanced up at the high rise before him. It looked like a rounded triangular column.

He stared at the sky above the building.

Small, white specks were fluttering down.

It had started snowing.

It was a fine, delicate snowfall.

A single flake, looking like a speck of dust on Takaki's coat collar, instantly vanished and seeped into the fabric.

It almost seemed as though the countless spots of light behind the high-rise windows were creating and dropping the substance.

The phone continued its low hum.

He couldn't answer Risa's call.

His fingers just wouldn't move.

"I love you, Risa."

The words just wouldn't come out.

Even though he felt so deeply for her.

Takaki wondered.

He thought he remembered feeling cornered like this long ago.

The frustration of not finding something important, no matter how hard he searched…

Yet his desire to embrace her would only intensify.

And before long, just reaching out became painful.

The vibration stopped.

Takaki thought:

Why don't I have the strength?

The strength to settle in one place.

The strength to deepen my attachment to someone.

The strength to love a human being.

The strength to carry a bit of someone else's pain on my shoulders.

Why don't I have that?

He was no rocket.

He was like a car with no engine.

He could only go downhill.

In which case…

When had he been at the top?

At what point did his time blithely crest the summit—

To turn into a side road that slowly made a mockery of it all?

11

Last night, she dreamed about the past.

Both he and Akari were still kids.

It had to be because of the letter she found yesterday.

Akari seemed to be the only passenger on the Ryomo Line train. Even when she sat straight up, she didn't see any heads sticking out above the green booths.

It was always empty at this time of day.

Outside the morning and evening rush hours, there were hardly ever any passengers onboard.

The train was making its way to Oyama Station, slowly.

Or perhaps she only felt that way due to the passing landscape's leisurely pace.

The paddies, packed with snow, subtly changed their orientations as they slid away.

Akari had used the line for all six years of her secondary schooling.

Although she was surveying familiar sights from a familiar train, something felt different, no doubt because her feelings differed from back then.

Trying to lean back on the hard, immovable seat just made her posture needlessly proper. So she'd turned to face the window. Her breath fogged up the glass.

This had to be what "ennui" felt like.

She sighed. When she rested her chin in her hand, her ring's gemstone pressed against her cheek.

I feel so fidgety, Akari thought.

Marriage was kind of strange.

She felt fidgety and so did everyone else.

Her parents actually seemed more flustered than her.

Akari had visited her parents' home to gather her things and was on her way back to Tokyo now that she was done. That was the sole reason for her trip, but her parents had insisted on seeing her off at the station as if it were a big deal.

It had been snowing on the platform in Iwafune. Icicles hung from the eaves of the station building, and the surrounding fields were dyed white.

She'd told her aging parents that they didn't have to, but they came anyway. They even went through the unmanned ticket gates to bid her farewell on the platform.

Akari had lived in Tokyo by herself for nearly ten years.

She was simply going back there, but her parents didn't see it that way.

"We wish you could stay until New Year's," her mother lamented.

"Me too…but there's still a lot left to do."

"Right. Cook something tasty for him too, okay?" her father said.

"I will."

"Call us if you need anything," her mother said.

"Got it," Akari answered with a wry smile.

The wind carried off each white puff of breath.

Around them, a snowy landscape.

It was like a scene out of a drama.

The similarity to cheesy TV made her want to giggle out of embarrassment, but she was touched nonetheless.

"We'll be seeing each other at my wedding in just a month, so could you stop worrying? Please, head back home and stay out of the cold," Akari begged with a grimace, but her voice might have been shaking a bit.

The train car's oscillations gave her a gentle shove.

Her left ring finger.

It still felt a bit strange. She hadn't gotten used to wearing a band on her left ring finger.

They say the finger is connected to the heart, and it did feel that way.

So, I'm getting married.

The fact had yet to sink in.

Living with him and being added to the family register was still a hazy notion, a prospect. Not so for the wedding preparations—they were an imminent, stressful reality.

Maybe she was trying to escape from it.

What kept coming back to her in that empty car were the early trains, nearly devoid of passengers, that she took to her middle school for morning basketball practice.

Often, in a booth she had all to herself, she'd place her stationery on her knees and write a letter.

She recalled her dream from last night.

In it, the street from the station gleamed white with snow under lonesome streetlamps.

It was a dream about a boy and a girl under that light leaving a pair of tracks on the cold, white, empty road and trekking into the dark.

Both of them were still kids.

It was a dream about the two wanting to become grownups soon, not being able to, and being painfully aware of it.

It had to be because of the letter she found yesterday.

Her first love letter.

The only one she ever wrote in her life, yet ended up keeping.

She found it tucked away in the back of her closet in an empty cookie can, along with the fancy stationery she used to write on, cassette tapes of her favorites songs, a graduation essay collection she didn't even want to look at. The letter was in a pink envelope. The seal had never been broken.

In the end, Akari opened it and read the whole thing. It was only after hesitating for some time.

Her old bedroom. Under its fluorescent light, dim from years of disuse, she could only close her eyes once she had finished.

Almost sweet, almost ticklish—Akane's heart trembled, and she was wrapped in it.

A few scenes came back to her: leaning against each other and reading the same book, running down the shrine path, and so on.

The train he took, that last day. She was riding the same line in the opposite direction.

The train seemed to be taking its time but was actually speeding towards its destination.

A little of how she'd felt back then revived in her.

From between a break in the clouds, light shone through the window.

Light fell on Akari's face.

It was bright.

She shut her eyes.

Surely, the mountain ridge was gleaming white in the light.

She could have sworn that there was a gentle breeze.

Ah.

She let out a deep sigh.

This is what your heart overflowing with emotion feels like.

10

After quitting his job, Takaki spent the days doing nothing.

He slept over ten hours a day and still felt drowsy, his head awfully numb.

He would wake up, lean against the wall, sit with his legs sticking straight out, and remain in that position. Turning on neither the lights nor any music.

He only went outside to buy random things to eat. It might be at midnight, or at dawn. He completely abandoned a proper daily cycle and lived instead like a wounded animal lying still in its den.

Apparently, he was more exhausted than he'd thought.

Takaki continued like this for about a month.

Then, at last, he was able to want to smoke again. He'd gone a whole month without a cigarette and not even noticed.

His fatigue wasn't gone, but he could move somewhat.

He went out to the veranda and lit a cigarette with a lighter.

How strange, he thought. *Filling my body with smoke clears my head.*

The cold February air pricked his skin, but he didn't have the energy to go back in and put on extra layers.

His fingertips hurt.

The hand holding the cigarette was shaking.

Takaki looked up.

He could see Shinjuku's high-rises not too far in the distance.

Numerous square towers rose to varied levels amidst a sprawling gray metropolis of low-crouching buildings.

Like cedars standing straight on a grassy field.

As if on a fast-forwarded video, clouds were pulling towards him.

Time suddenly seemed to be flowing again.

He must have hoped that time would grind to a halt while he was curled up in his room.

Maybe it balanced out the years he spent on fast forward.

From now on, he wasn't going anywhere. Nothing would happen. How relieved he'd be if Earth cut out its rotating and revolving.

But...he supposed that was a tall order.

No matter how much he ran in circles or stood still, a month was a month, a second a second.

What a depressing conclusion...

His own thoughts made Takaki sigh.

Actually, way back when, didn't I wish time would pass more quickly, so I'd become an adult right away? Didn't I with all my heart?

When was that, and why did I feel that way?

It was at that moment that "the dream" came back to him.

He wasn't sure if it was that morning, or some time ago, but he did have the dream.

It always faded from his memory upon waking, but out of the blue, he'd remembered. A dream he used to have when he was a kid.

Ah, yes. Takes me back...

Just then—he received a message on his cell phone.

Even without opening the message, he felt he knew who it was from and what it said.

Pressing that button was going to take some courage.

Takaki went back in from the veranda.

His cell phone was flashing orange on the low table.

He was really nervous. He hadn't checked his emails in a while. He simply hadn't wanted to interact with anyone.

Takaki just stood there staring at his phone, as if that might pause his time and annul everything.

But the light on his mobile kept blinking in his dark room. Relentlessly, as if to remind him that time was wasting…

He picked it up.

He pressed the button.

The words jumped out at him.

For a moment his mind seemed unwilling to recognize them.

Hello, Takaki.

So the words said.

Hello, Takaki.

It's been a while.

How have you been?

I've been going back and forth about it for a while now, but there's something I just have to say.

"Sometimes it feels like your eyes look right through me, the view from the window, the food on the table, and out at something formless, like at a concept or idea. That's all that I know. When you're looking through things it feels as if you're trying to make yourself fade away and disappear."

Her message was very, very long.

He scrolled down, line by line.

When he finished reading and glanced up from his phone, it felt as if all of the color had faded from everything in sight.

He had known "this moment" would come but was hoping he could delay it just a little while more.

Suddenly every object in his room that made up his daily life seemed coated in a layer of dust.

Even his wrinkled bedsheets, the toothbrush in his bathroom, and the history on his cell phone.

Everything announced that she was gone.

He straightened the collar of his overcoat, put on his boots, and left his apartment.

The metallic blast of the closing steel door resounded in his ears.

When he turned the key, the cold click of the lock clawed at his chest.

He pushed the button and waited for the elevator.

The rising numbers on the display felt urgent and oppressive.

When the thick, automatic double doors opened to reveal an empty box, he almost felt wounded.

Barely able to stand during his short ride to the first floor lobby, he leaned, or rather collapsed against the wall.

The motor's hum annoyed him…

There was a metallic sound.

His keys had slipped out of his hand.

He looked at the floor.

His key holder had fallen.

He couldn't pick it up.

Three keys were attached to it.

The key to his apartment, the key to his bicycle, and…

He wanted to direct his eyes elsewhere.

He inhaled.

He slowly bent down and picked up his key holder.

Even that small act required great willpower.

He left his apartment building and came to Ome Highway.

He tried his hardest not to slouch as he strolled in the heart of town. It was busy with passing vehicles.

The chilly air penetrating his coat wouldn't stop whispering to him

214

in a language he didn't understand.

All of the muscles in his body were cooling. They felt heavy, as if they were freezing solid.

He walked by the fence of a vacant lot.

Two yellow cranes hunched over in their parking spots.

Perhaps the lot would become a new building.

Red and white headlights. Passing strangers. Lit signs. Noise.

While Takaki burned with such agony, the townscape threw him an indifferent look as it went about its daily life.

His heart smarted as if that apathy were filing it down.

He hated how everything around him looked back at him with a blank expression.

Sure, it was just reflecting his own.

Even so.

It would be such a lifesaver if someone asked him what was wrong right about now.

Just as she had approached him out of the blue on the platform long ago.

"I still love you," Risa, the woman he'd dated for three years, wrote in her email. "But in spite of the thousand messages we've sent each other, our hearts only grew closer by an inch."

She's right, Takaki thought. *And it's my fault.*

Nonetheless, it was the only path he could have chosen. The only way it could have turned out. As a person he just wasn't designed to steer with ease. He could only go straight. He'd chosen to live in this manner, in this town. The world was the world, scenery was scenery, and he was himself. Didn't he decide one day to go ahead on his own and never get too involved?

Reflecting off the frame of a bicycle parked by the road, the low light of evening leapt into his eyes.

He could feel his brow crease.

He averted his eyes.

The slanting rays shone on just the top half of apartment buildings.
A blue sign that gave directions hung above a main road.
Lit up by the setting sun, it was illegible.
Where was he headed anyway?

It's just like you said, Risa.
The closer you came, the more I distanced myself.
But if that's true, why should getting your farewell message make me feel so terrible?

9

She was still thinking about last night's dream.
Set in those bygone days.
In it, the two of them were still thirteen—

Akari got off the aging train car, green and orange, at Oyama Station. She took an underground passage, and when she arrived at the platform for Ueno, tiny snowflakes were fluttering down from the sky.
The snow likely wouldn't stick. She checked the display, but it didn't look like there were going to be any suspensions in service.
What perfect timing, Akari thought.
She couldn't help remembering various things.
That day, too, it had snowed.
A snowstorm.
The trains had stopped.
That day, fourteen years ago, Takaki had stood on the very same platform, buffeted by a wintry storm.
He must have glanced up at the same display a hundred times over.
Until that day, Akari hadn't known that trains sometimes stopped running when it snowed.

He must have been under the same impression.

She looked at the sky, clouded white. Then she watched the specks of snow tumbling down one after another fairly rapidly.

Having grown up in Tochigi, she was used to the sight, but it was still oddly unsettling and made her anxious.

He must have felt the same way.

Akari tried to leap across time and picture the station as it had been fourteen years ago.

A boy stood still with snowflakes clinging to his duffle coat.

She couldn't recall his face clearly anymore.

Yet somehow his air, breath, and mood, recovered from her heart, played on the screen of her conscious mind.

At a gray station where the trains weren't running, a thirteen-year-old boy stubbornly clenched his fist in the face of anxiety and panic.

He'd endured all of that bitter pain just to meet thirteen-year-old Akari Shinohara.

Like a gemstone.

How beautiful.

When he finally arrived at midnight, after countless stoppages on a single track, the area around Iwafune Station was buried in white.

The two of them walked under the sparse streetlamps.

Beyond the station front spread fields covered in snow—

Scattered house lights gleaming only in the distance—

If they ever looked back, their footprints were the only marks in the thick new snow.

While the real Akari was immersed in her past on the Oyama platform, a silver train pulled in.

She readjusted the bag on her shoulder.

On that night when they were both thirteen, just for the two of them, the fluttering snow had been cherry petals.

—And so, he and I believed…

The train slowly decelerated.

A set of doors stopped right in front of Akari.

—without a speck of doubt…

The automatic doors opened.

—that we would see the cherry blossoms together again someday.

Right then Akari could almost see a young boy in a navy duffle coat rushing out of the train and onto the platform…

8

Takaki realized that it had gotten dark while he aimlessly wandered the streets.

He had no specific destination in mind, he was just walking. He had somehow made his way to Shinjuku proper and figured he hadn't left the town. He could tell by his surroundings.

Passing by other pedestrians now and then, he kept pressing forward in a mixed-occupancy area that wasn't quite downtown or business district.

The faint light from a convenience store spilled onto the streets on his left. Without thinking too deeply, he entered.

If you roamed around at night, a convenience store sucked you in sooner or later. It was like a light trap.

In college, students gathered in the cafeteria when they had nothing to do, and maybe convenience stores were the labor force's lunchrooms. You could get something to eat and even skim through some magazines for the time being.

Takaki was drawn to the magazine section along the window.

He picked out a copy of *Science Magazine* and flipped through it. He didn't want to read it in particular, he just wasn't interested in any of the other ones. He was simply trying to distract himself.

He restlessly turned the colored pages.

His hand stopped.

The universe jumped out at him.

More accurately, it was a photo of outer space.

Tiny stars were scattered across a black sky. On the right side of the centerfold floated a spacecraft with a giant parabolic antenna. It appeared to be floating, but the thing was probably hurtling at a cosmic speed.

The headline declared that the ELISH Space Probe was taking its first step beyond the solar system.

Takaki read the article. The Japanese space probe ELISH, launched in 1999, had achieved a final swing-by around Neptune and embarked on its eternal journey to the end of the universe. Just as you might hook your hand on a corner and turn with that centrifugal force, a "swing-by" took advantage of a celestial body's gravitational pull to fling a vessel deeper into space.

After its final swing-by around Neptune, ELISH would rely solely on inertia to continue its endless flight away from the solar system. As long as its atomic battery kept working, for approximately twenty years ELISH would continue to transmit data to Earth. The probe wouldn't be returning to the solar system afterwards. To see just how much distance it might put between itself and its place of birth—really, for no other reason—ELISH would be advancing straight into literal emptiness, forever.

Takaki casually returned to the spread and its CGI image of space.

Which is to say…

It'll rarely meet even a single hydrogen atom.

Chills suddenly shot up his spine.

Once they subsided, he realized what had brought them on.

"Him."

That guy.

The orange light that climbed the sky on the island that night.

The rocket Takaki and Kanae gazed up at.

In 1999—

So it had gotten that far?

It was all coming back to Takaki.

Twilight… The air felt different. As if there had been a blackout. He'd felt something and turned towards it. The ascending light. The column of smoke. The delayed vibrations…

That time. He'd felt himself change.

No.

He simply accepted what he was to become.

He'd forge into the unknown with his eyes shut.

He learned that about himself.

Takaki understood it was all he could do, after witnessing *him*.

"I see…"

He had gone that far, over eight years?

Right now, Takaki was at a standstill.

Probably for the first time since seeing the rocket at Tanegashima that day, he'd stopped moving.

And he felt guilty…

That space probe—that rocket—pushed forward without a moment's hesitation and was already past Neptune.

He, the rocket, not even given a final destination, was following an order to "go as far as you can wherever that may be" and continuing his uniform linear motion.

He was only a machine, yet Takaki trembled at his strength.

He'd end up somewhere. Though Takaki didn't know where, surely it was someplace worth going.

Just the way he spent eight years reaching Neptune—he would

arrive at an unknown place over an eternity.

While Takaki just stood here…

—*No, that's not true.*

At that moment, it hit him.

Ahh…

The gentle feeling in the pit of his stomach spread to his whole body.

It wasn't that he ended up in this place.

He had arrived here.

This wasn't who he wanted to be. But he was here.

This wasn't where he wanted to find himself. But he'd arrived here.

So this was Neptune.

—*I finally got this far.*

It wasn't where he was trying to go.

But he had walked all the way here on his own two feet.

The debt and deficit weighing on him began to fade. Untangling from his shoulders and feet, it retreated.

He returned the magazine to its rack.

He took a step back, then headed toward the exit.

He thought about "the dream" he'd miraculously remembered that morning.

He had dreamed.

About the past.

About his past self.

—*In it, the two of us were still thirteen…*

Takaki walked.

He could feel his steps on the white floor.

—In the dream spread fields covered in snow…
—our footprints the only marks in the thick new snow.

Now, every time Takaki took a step forward, he felt a pleasant one g.

In those days…

He had wanted to grow taller, right away. To reach higher, right away.

He'd wanted to be strong for real.

The boy in his dream—his past self—sincerely wished for those things.

That strength was now here.

He was the person he once longed to be.

Once, when just for the two of them, the fluttering snow had been cherry petals.

—She and I believed, without a speck of doubt…

Takaki grasped distances much better than he used to—

And he could pick up and handle many more things.

Even if his one desire from back then was no longer within reach.

—that we would see the cherry blossoms together again someday.

That day, he'd wanted to become bigger and stronger.

And now it was all here. In him.

He faced the door to the outside world.

7

The automatic doors opened.

Akari stepped onto the train to Tokyo.

6

The automatic doors opened.

Takaki stepped into the raging winds of February.

5

> I'm always searching for you,
> In my dreams and at the crosswalk,
> Even though I know you're not there.
>
> If a miracle were to occur,
> I'd want to show you now,
> This new morning, who I'll be from now on,
> And the words "I love you" that I couldn't say.
>
> "One more time, One more chance"
> —lyrics by Masayoshi Yamazaki

4

Takaki Tohno surveyed Shinjuku, the town where he lived, as if he were seeing it for the very first time. He filled his lungs with the cold air. He stretched his neck. He realized he'd been hanging his head when he walked.

He breathed in, then out.

The white puff of breath floated away.

He was here.

He walked.

The colors of the landscape flew into his consciousness and then out again. They left something in him.

It was still snowing. He wanted it to snow a whole lot more.

Takaki evaded the oncoming stream of people as he walked through the busy night streets.

The radiance and commotion of downtown.

The smell and presence of human beings.

Neon signs.

The clear outline of the high-rise buildings.

The blurred light of the traffic signals.

Various faces coming and going.

An assortment of outfits.

Illuminated signs. Wind. Roadside trees. Fallen leaves.

The fallen leaves from the roadside trees twirled in the wind as if they were taking dance steps and brushed against the electronic billboards before falling to the ground.

Takaki's optic nerves registered everything as light. That light was building something in his heart.

He crossed the crosswalk.

He stopped in the middle of the road.

He glanced up at the snowy sky reflecting the city lights.

The endless snow looked as if it was radiating from a single point in the sky.

He watched a bird fly across the night sky.

The pattern of the pavement on the sidewalk.

The guardrail.

He approached a construction site.

The shadow of the mobile cranes, huddled together on an unfinished building.

The station's worn staircase.

The automatic ticket gates.

He peered down at the road from the platform.

Taillights created a river of illumination.

He returned to his apartment.

He leapt into bed and fell into a deep sleep.

And he had a dream.

About his younger days. His childhood. His middle school years. Events from high school played back on his mental screen.

His memory of running through the trees in Nagano ceded to a memory of passing through a city shrine. While those sensations still lingered inside him, he felt himself speeding uphill on his bicycle in Tanegashima.

He remembered several friends who'd left deep impressions on him. He remembered each of the few girls who'd reached out to touch his heart.

The memory of Kanae's soft arms and lean shoulders floated into his mind.

He recalled the day he left for Tokyo.

When Takaki arrived at Tanegashima Airport with a heavy bag hanging off his shoulder, Kanae was there to see him off.

Without saying anything of much importance, he uttered a casual "all right, then" and went through the gates.

That felt as bitter as chewing metal.

He remembered the cold-hearted, noble beauty he met at his part-time job as a cram school instructor.

He wished he could meet her one more time.

Risa's simple gestures and kind voice.

The tickle he got in the back of his throat whenever he heard her voice revived in him.

Immersed in a warm darkness, he took his time savoring the cross-current of memories.

He woke up.

He went down the stairs and out of his apartment building.

He took in the morning air.

He started wandering around.

Even after a good night's sleep, the images of reality that flew into his eyes were intoxicating.

Dawn's rays shone on each tidy structure in a residential district.

The sun rose over a fenced-off uphill road.

A gentle light filtered into a modest park.

He felt the world through his skin.

The world of memories in him blended and became one with the world that was here now.

Various memories.

He crossed a big old stone bridge. The city's memories were older than Takaki knew. He stopped in the middle of the bridge and peered down at the river.

The water shimmered with light.

He suddenly remembered the sea.

How the landscape abruptly broke off on his right to reveal a vast sea as he rode his Cub home on the national highway.

He went under an overpass.

He saw a bicycle with a basket leaning against a concrete wall. Beyond it, thin clouds hung in a bright, spacious sky.

A traffic sign cast a bent shadow over the curb.

A high-school girl, carrying a sports bag on her shoulder, hurried down the street.

A patch of clear weather spread across the city sky.

Sunlight reflected off the edges of the river flowing through the city.

He entered a station-front bakery that opened early in the morning and drank coffee in its café.

He sat by a big window where he had a view of the street outside. For hours, he gently gazed at the flow of people going to school and to work.

When he stepped out of the café, the winter air had become softer and more pleasant.

He randomly felt the urge to pass through the terrace at Shinjuku Station's southern exit.

Climbing the small staircase up from Shinjuku Station, he arrived at a spacious promenade that gleamed white in the sunlight.

He stopped in the middle.

The promenade was wide enough for a few traffic lanes if it were meant for cars, and a smattering of people passed him from the back and the front.

Others sat idly on the rims of flowerbeds and were enjoying the breeze.

Gradually veering to the left, Takaki leaned against the handrail that ran along the path.

When he looked down from the edge of the raised southern terrace, he saw the JR Line. It was just like peering down at a river from a bridge.

He gazed at the trains flowing in and out.

The wind blew.

The sky was a fresh, light blue.

Low in the corner, the Docomo Tower, reminiscent of a medieval clock tower, poked its head out a bit hazily.

A white petal, from what flower Takaki couldn't tell, came dancing in the wind from somewhere and tried to flit past his eyes.

He reached out.

The petal obediently settled into his hand.

Takaki held it softly, dearly, careful not to crush it.

He recalled catching a cherry petal like that in the spring as a high schooler.

Cherry blossoms bloomed even on Tanegashima.

The warm island air came back to life in him.

He remembered gazing up into the massive sky.

Tanegashima's refreshing blue summer sky.

That deep blue had once tugged at his heartstrings.

Even now he felt as if he could smell the grass.

His heart flew to a faint-green hill.

The swaying grass.

The smell of soil carrying on the breeze.

The scent of the tide.

Far below the hill, a bluish-black sea.

The whitecaps.

The sun, white too and strong, warmed his body.

Dazzling.

Hot.

Enough to melt his consciousness.

His mind spun.

Surrounded by the world.

Enveloped.

Cradled.

The flying birds.

The lovely, nameless wildflowers.

The winged insects that hopped from one flower to the next.

He peered down at the wide Tanegashima plains from the hill.

The dark green of the forested mountains. The gentle green of the sugarcane fields. The fresh leaves of Tanegashima sweet potatoes in orderly lines. The red soil. The blue sky. Bright, fraying clouds. The swaying windbreaks.

The light was hot.

The wind was hot.

The turning windmill.

That landscape came rushing back to him from the furthest reaches of his memory.

He felt like crying.

The island had been so beautiful.

Why hadn't he ever noticed?

So pretty.

So pretty.

It had seemed obvious, but he had never really noticed.

He had been blessed.

He looked back.

He looked up.

He spun.

The world spun.

Everything spun, like a nebula, and gathered to Takaki.

He was at the center of the universe.

3

They were married at the end of winter, and now it was cherry blossom season.

Their new life was picture-perfect even from Akari's own perspective.

They'd moved into an apartment in Kichijoji. It was fairly old and cramped, but also quite cozy. Its small size gave home and resident a chance to grow close.

True, her husband often grimaced when he thought about their loan payments.

Akari continued to work despite her marriage. She saw no reason to quit a job that she loved.

"I want to hear you bark, 'Which is more important, me or your job?'" she joked. He laughed heartily and said he looked forward to asking that. Of course, Akari had no intention of ever making him say something so sad and tedious. He wouldn't, either, which was why they could laugh about it.

That made her happy.

Since her husband was awful at cooking and doing laundry, Akari had no choice but to handle those chores. He was certainly capable of pushing buttons on a washing machine but was a lost cause when it came to folding clothes.

Yet he always made sure to iron his own shirts. What's more, he was pretty good at it. It seemed to be one of those things that some guys were picky about. Akari didn't quite get it.

Her husband took care of all cleaning and dishwashing duties to balance things out. Apparently those two activities suited his nature and didn't bother him at all. A godsend for Akari.

I can make dinner without worrying about the dishes. This is heaven!

Be that as it may, when the time was right, she was going to teach him how to fold clothes at least. It wouldn't hurt if he also learned how to make simple side dishes and rice porridge.

It was a Saturday and Akari had the day off from work.

Her husband had left in the morning thanks to a business matter that required some extra attention. He was having to work over the weekend during their honeymoon period, but he just loved his job, and he'd walked out the door in high spirits.

Akari felt quite cheery, too, as she hung the laundry out on the veranda to dry.

The weather was lovely.

Their home was sparkling clean thanks to her husband's diligent efforts the day before, so she was in a particularly good mood.

Akari was enjoying her life, both at work and at home.

It was all so fulfilling.

Hm?

Wait.

Just then, a notion seemed to sprout in her chest. Something nagged at her.

It was as if she'd forgotten an important promise.

Maybe she'd borrowed an item that was important to someone and wasn't remembering.

Standing vacantly on her veranda, she ended up looking out at the scenery.

Some small thing danced before her eyes.

It was a cherry petal, fluttering by from somewhere. She tried to catch it but was too slow. It neatly slipped out of her hand.

Perhaps it was the petal that enticed her.

She felt like going to see the cherry blossoms.

She started heading to Yoyogi Park.

2

Takaki started a new job.

That being said, programming was his only meal ticket. He'd focused on that one skill as a working member of society. He knew he could make it just about anywhere in that field, though.

He asked some industry acquaintances from his time at the company if they could send along any odd jobs that he could do on his own now that he'd quit. Despite the recession and Takaki's low expectations, they had a few projects for him right away.

At a meeting, one of them bluntly told Takaki, "You've got the skills, though I don't know about your personality." They both had a good laugh over that. When a different acquaintance made a direct offer to try to recruit him, Takaki felt he had no choice but to politely decline.

He moved to a 2K apartment in Shibuya.

He purchased a high-end Apple machine and the parts to build himself a Windows PC and brought in a wide desk and an Aeron chair to turn one of his rooms into an office. He put in an order for his business cards and started working as a freelance programmer.

His new lifestyle where he worked at his own pace, chose his jobs, and just kept an eye on his deadlines was comfortable.

Sometimes he received sudden spec changes, and having to comply felt absurd, but he learned to take it in stride and not let it bother him too much (though it did sometimes get to him).

He set his own break times. He worked through the night when he felt like it.

He'd been liberated. Gravity no longer grew stronger, or weaker.

Due to some whim that even Takaki couldn't comprehend, he actually started using his kitchen. He prepared three meals for himself every day. So he could, if he tried! He replaced his old refrigerator because he needed a bigger freezer.

He bought bookshelves and a storage rack and organized his room. Previously, he never wanted to waste his time on things like that.

Takaki ran a check on his 24-inch screen, removed his hands from the keyboard, and stretched back in his chair.

He had worked through the night, and it was ten in the morning.

The delicate aroma of spring drifted into his room from the open window.

The curtains swayed.

As if whisked away by the warm spring wind, Takaki stepped outside.

1

Now that she thought about it, that nagging feeling predated her wedding. She'd assumed it was just the marriage blues.

But was it something else?

Somewhere deep down, did she regret getting married?

Akane burst out laughing. *Nah.*

She transferred from the Inokashira Line to the Odakyu at Shimo-kitazawa and got off at Yoyogi-Uehara. She would walk from there.

She was shocked that simply getting married could make her feel so fulfilled.

Her quick steps made clacking sounds.

Her skin faintly warm in the radiant sunshine, she thought she might doze off even as she walked.

She came to a crossing that looked charming enough to serve as a location for a movie or TV drama. It was incredibly wide sideways.

Houses lined the tracks, and potted plants filled gardens that were too small to be called such. They shone a beautiful bright green in the spring sun.

Yoyogi Park's luxurious greenery was visible on the other side of the crossing.

A great cherry tree stood right beside the crossing signal.

Not a single leaf had sprouted yet.

It was in full bloom.

The tall branches were dyed a soft, light pink. The petals gently reflected the sunlight, making the tree glow like a big standing lamp.

Petals fell from the blossoms and, tossed by the wind, danced over the tracks and crossing.

Akari entered it amidst the fluttering petals.

When she had gone about a third of the way, the warning started to sound. From the looks of it, the gate would come down shortly after she was done crossing. She didn't need to hasten her pace.

It was a truly picturesque scene.

It looks just like snow, Akari thought.

The warm air felt nice. She felt so relaxed her heart could melt. She spaced out a little.

Then Akari passed someone.

0

People tend to think that I've got my head in the clouds, but my emotions are actually pretty extreme. It's obvious if I'm being serious or not. When I'm thinking about the person I like, or when he is in front of me, I space out so badly that I almost lose my mind. Contemplating all sorts of things and writhing in pain, anguish, anger, I log in the corner of my heart a lot of stuff that I could never say while I'm sober. But I'm different when I cool down. I calmly deal with my work and daily life in all their detail. There's a part of me that handles things in

233

a composed and realistic manner. My hots and colds are as fierce as a desert. I would be perfectly normal if I could just balance them out.

My own power surprises me when my switch is on. I find myself falling in love with such passion. Sometimes I wonder where all that empathic energy is coming from.

Right…

It's really important, and the key to living. The reason I've managed to survive.

Actually looking at someone. Being looked at in return. Trying to enter each other's hearts. Trying to understand someone. Yearning to be understood.

Long ago, at a certain moment one day, I discovered that wonderful experience.

Life isn't all sunshine and rainbows. Sometimes it's like vomiting blood. The pain seems out to wring all the fluids from your body. But even in those trying times, I always felt protected. Even when I was bitterly betrayed by someone I had trusted, even when I was hurt much worse, even when things got so complicated in high school that I had to hide out alone at lunchtime.

I was protected. I kept receiving that power. In a corner of my heart, when things got really tough, I could always sense an endlessly benevolent, mysterious presence carrying half my burdens on its shoulders.

That presence, in fact, was always with me. It stayed close beside me. Behind the mailbox when I quickly glanced at it, in the back-alley window, and on the facing platform—it was always wherever my heart was.

Which is why I was okay.

I never felt lonely.

1

The instant Takaki passed the woman in the middle of the crossing, a momentous and fatal realization came upon him.

He understood everything. That overwhelming recognition hit Takaki like a ton of bricks. And yet he couldn't reproduce his understanding on a conscious level. He had obtained all of the answers but couldn't put them into words.

Emotions and memories that he had never been able to organize, the chaos he carried in himself, clanged loudly, reassembled, detached, transformed, and fell into place.

The phantasmal horizon over which a binary star ascended in Takaki contracted, to a single point like so many grains of sand, and shattered. The sparkling powder dispersed, and turned into snow, and gathered on a window frame. A halted train. A dark, snowy landscape. Time frozen. Time and space, frozen, extended into another dimension. A rocket turned into a building, the building converted into lines of code, and the lines of code crystallized. All of his emotions condensed into transparent crystal—

Which shattered to pieces.

Being shot in the head without seeing it coming must feel the same.

Cherry petals twirled.

Like they were the fragments of his burst emotions.

Confusion.

Some baffling force coerced him.

Takaki just kept on walking.

The warning still sounded.

—If he turned around, surely she would too.

He was past the crossing now. The gate descended behind him. He stopped walking.

—He was sure of it.

He turned around.

The woman, faced away from him, slowly started to turn.

At last, her profile

Just then an Odakyu train came hurtling in from the left with an ear-splitting noise. Rushing by at a ferocious speed, it blocked Takaki's view. Silver cars marked with blue stripes kept flowing over the tracks like a river and kept separating him from the passerby like a wall.

The train was very, very long.

On the other side, a woman.

The train was taking forever.

It was like a blaring wall of sound. He couldn't hear a thing.

Soon.

It would soon pass.

The moment he thought it was gone, another train came speeding in from the right to obstruct his view.

He couldn't see.

He couldn't see her.

The wind from the speeding train buffeted him.

He put one foot behind him and entered into a slight crouch without thinking.

Ah, if this were a few months ago, I might have dashed into the crossing and gotten myself killed.

The second train passed, leaving behind an echo and faint after-image.

The crossing signal stopped sounding.

The gate began to rise.

The thick spring air, the sun's gold-tinted rays—petals gently dancing over the tracks.

The pink presence of the cherry tree beside the crossing signal.

Within that scenery—

The woman had vanished.

Petals were swept up by the wind.

Oddly enough, a smile appeared on his face.

Why did he feel so fulfilled when she hadn't turned around?

He asked her a question in his mind.

What in the world did you just give to me?

While he had only glimpsed her profile, he could tell that she was pretty.

There was something about her. Yes, an aura of happiness, the fulfillment that she felt, seemed to rush over him like a wave.

Good.

Good vibes.

It was great seeing someone who seemed happy. It somehow made him feel generous too. He wanted to pass along the kindness.

It was funny, how strong he felt.

He had this sense that he could tackle something new.

2

Takaki turned away from the crossing and started walking.

The warm air felt nice. He felt so relaxed his heart could melt.

Now, what might he do?

Nothing was beyond him.

Maybe he should try calling someone.

Who?

Anyone, really.

As long as he knew their number, he could connect to them. He could talk to anyone.

He had forgotten his cell at home.

Was there a phone booth around here?

He'd take a little look around.

Right.

He could go anywhere.

Takaki stepped forth—

And turned a corner.

Dear Takaki,

How have you been?

We never thought there would be a snowstorm on the day we promised to meet, did we? The trains seem to be delayed. Which is why I decided to write this while I wait for you.

There's a stove in front of me, so it's warm here. And I always keep stationery in my bag. It's so I can write to you any time I want. I'm thinking about giving you this letter later on, so I would be pretty flustered if you got here too soon. There's no rush, so please take your time.

Today will be the first day that we've met in a while. I can't believe it's been eleven months. So I'm honestly a little nervous. I'm even worried that we might not recognize each other. Still, the station here is much smaller than any in Tokyo, so it would be impossible for us to miss each other. No matter how hard I try to picture you in your new school uniform or soccer clothes, it feels like I'm imagining someone I don't know.

I'm going to write down all of the things that I could never tell you properly.

You really saved me when I transferred to Tokyo in fourth grade. I was so happy that I could be your friend. I think school would have been a nightmare if it hadn't been for you.

That was why I couldn't bear the thought of transferring away. I wanted us to go to the same junior high and grow up together. I'd always wished we could. I've gotten used to the middle school here, somehow (so please don't worry), but I keep on thinking how great it'd be if you were with me, many times a day.

It hurts to know that you're going to move to so far away. Even though Tokyo and Tochigi aren't exactly close, I always figured I could find you if I had to. I could see you right away if I just hopped on a train. But the other side of Kyushu is just too far away.

From now on, I have to learn how to make it on my own. I'm not very confident that I can.

But there's something that I need to tell you. I might not be able to say it out loud today, so I'll write it down in this letter.

I love you, Takaki. I don't remember when I started loving you. It just naturally happened before I knew it. You were so strong and kind from the first time I met you. You always protected me.

You are going to be okay, Takaki. No matter what happens, I know you will grow up to be a wonderful, kindhearted person. No matter how far away from me you go, I'll absolutely still love you.

Please, please remember that.

＊　　＊　　＊　　＊　　＊　　＊　　＊

Dear Akari,

How are you? It's nine p.m. and I'm writing this in my room. I can see tiny building lights outside my window. What do you see out of yours right now? It's a little hard for me to imagine.

I really should be doing my math homework, but lately I've been slacking off a lot. None of my friends in soccer club take homework seriously, and I don't really feel like doing it when I think about how I'll be moving soon.

We're going to meet in two weeks, right? I'm thinking of giving you this letter then.

I hear the island on the other side of Kyushu that I'll be moving to is super rural, but that it also has a NASDA launch site. That's the only part of moving that I'm excited about. I'll tell you all about the awesome launch after I've seen it. At this point, that's all I really have to look forward to.

Honestly, I'm anxious about moving so far away. I just want to be an adult already. Right now, I feel stuck at a weird age. I'm just realizing that I should have gone to see you sooner. I don't know why I didn't. There are so many things I've been wanting to tell you since I started junior high. I've been missing you this entire time. I love you, Akari.

I still don't know what growing up is all about.

But, if we happen to meet again, someday in the distant future, I want to be someone that you can be proud of.

I want to make you that promise, Akari.